THE DEVIL'S TRAMPING GROUND

and Other North Carolina Mystery Stories

The Devil's Tramping Ground

AND OTHER
NORTH CAROLINA
MYSTERY STORIES

by JOHN HARDEN

Originator of
"TALES OF TAR HEELIA"

With drawings by
MARY LINDSAY McALISTER

Chapel Hill

THE UNIVERSITY OF NORTH CAROLINA PRESS

Copyright © 1949 by
The University of North Carolina Press
All rights reserved
Manufactured in the United States of America
ISBN 0-8078-0561-0
Library of Congress Catalog Card Number 49-4259

First printing, May 1949
Second printing, November 1949
Third printing, April 1953
Fourth printing, January 1957
Fifth printing, December 1964
Sixth printing, October 1966
Seventh printing, July 1969
Eighth printing, November 1972

To

''MUDDIES''

forever a Virginian, who taught
her large family of North Carolinians
to love their State

Preface

THIS VOLUME is an outgrowth of a weekly radio program presented for sixteen months over Radio Station WPTF at Raleigh, North Carolina, in 1946 and 1947. The radio series was called "Tales of Tar Heelia," and it gave me the opportunity of indulging in a hobby—the collection and preservation of unusual North Carolina stories. As I told my stories each week over the air, there developed from listeners a demand for many of the stories in some lasting and usable form.

And there is a genuine need for such collection, or preservation, of North Carolina's rich supply of legends, historical incidents, and folklore. These are important as a means of providing a permanent record of the background for the larger story of our state, her people, and their times. Through these we can have a better understanding of our tradition, a greater pride in our past, a broader consciousness of our heritage and culture, and a keener appreciation of our regional and national character.

These stories are perishable—just how perishable I have found as I have dug for some of these yarns. There is always a limited time for recording something of the moving stream, and a number of our better stories have already been lost or garbled. So we have a responsibility in this respect. There are older people in our state who know first-hand the stories, the legends of our state. With their passing may go even the memory of much of our wonderful story heritage.

I was frankly surprised at the spontaneous demand that appeared in connection with my radio presentation of these stories—seeking for them some more permanent recording. The call came from school, library, playground, and camp people, as well as from a rather astonishing cross section of interested individuals.

Over the radio, the story series included North Carolina mysteries, ghost stories, adventure stories, folk tales, and unusual yarns about unusual things in the state's story background. From these, for this volume, the mysteries have been segregated into a group. Our North Carolina ghost stories, adventure stories, and so on, might well form their own collections.

Tar Heelia has more than its share of mysteries, historical and otherwise. The history of the region that is today North

Carolina started out with an unsolved mystery—the lost colony of Roanoke Island. Other North Carolina stories, not so universally known but just as interesting, offer mysteries quite as fascinating and equally baffling. At least one of these stories has never before been written. So I bring together something of the old and something of the new, something of the known as well as of the unknown, in a rather comprehensive collection of mystery stories of North Carolina. The range embraces acts of violence, beautiful poetry, graceful animals, delicate shrubs, phantom lights, and many things in the behavior of man and nature that come and go without understanding or explanation.

Here, for the first time, the better-known mystery stories of North Carolina are assembled in one place, between one set of covers, for the convenience of those who have an interest in them. In the past it has been necessary to go to as many different sources as there are stories to get any light on these fascinating mystery tales of Tar Heelia.

I owe credit to Richard Mason and Graham Poyner, manager and program director of Radio Station WPTF at the time these yarns were developed in their original form. Assistant Director Porter Cowles and Virginia Reynolds of the editorial staff of the University of North Carolina Press guided this effort with their skilled touch, from the rewriting of radio scripts to the completion of the volume you hold in your hands. And no one writes of North Carolina without help at one place or another from Bill Sharpe, the press agent that Irvin S. Cobb said North Carolina needed. I am pleased to have the book illustrated by Mary Lindsay McAlister of Salisbury, a rising young artist of exceptional talent. At this writing she is still in art school perfecting herself for a fine career that lies ahead. To be sure I have my daughter—and the friendship that exists between her and Mary Lindsay McAlister—to thank for the young artist's services here.

With these, I also pay tribute to, and express my gratitude for, North Carolina's humble raconteurs of legend and story who have kept many of these stories alive down through the years and to those who brought this book into being through their expressed desire for a collection of North Carolina mysteries.

The stories embrace our state from the capes to the coves, from Palmettos to the land of the Potomac. They are all a part of the weaving in of the warp of our state's story, and I present them as such.

—*John Harden*

Greensboro, North Carolina
October 2, 1948

Contents

THE DEVIL'S TRAMPING GROUND

and Other North Carolina Mystery Stories

The Ghost Ship Mystery of Diamond Shoals

~~~~~~

M ANY weird puzzles exist in the seafaring history of
Eastern North Carolina. Legends of ships and men
abound along our colorful Tar Heel coast country. For the
locale of this ghost ship mystery we go to the Hatteras section
of the Outer Banks, long known to the men of the sea as "the
graveyard of ships."

It was a midwinter morning in February, 1921, and the
gray light of a waking dawn edged up over the rim of the
Atlantic. The first rays pointed ominously to North Carolina's Cape Hatteras shore. There, on the outer Diamond
Shoals—dreaded by seamen the world over—was a strange

sight. A five-masted schooner, under full sail with her prow cut deep in the sand, was heaving mightily against the restraining land.

The morning watch at the near-by Cape Hatteras coast guard station was momentarily stunned by the eerie spectacle. There had been no storm. The last watch to scan the shore and sea before darkness closed in the night before had reported all clear and calm, with neither sail nor smoke in sight. No light had been shown during the night, and no distress signals had been sent up.

What ship was this? Where did she come from? How could she possibly have grounded? Why had not the crew given some sign of the ship's distress?

But the coast guard acts as it questions, and a power lifeboat, launched at the Hatteras station, soon pulled up on the strange craft stuck firmly there on the Diamond Shoals. The coastguardmen found that the ship was the *Carroll M. Deering,* a new and apparently seaworthy vessel. Her spreading sails, set full to catch the wind, were of new cloth. But no one greeted the coastguardmen from the deck. Her jibs and topsails, still unfurled, indicated that there had been no attempt to float the ship off the shoals.

The rescue boat could get no nearer to the nest of shoals than a quarter of a mile because the sea was running strong; so the little coast guard crew studied the *Carroll M. Deering* from a distance. They noted that she seemed to be stripped of her lifeboats and that a ladder hung over her port side. The rescuers estimated that the ship would have a crew of at least ten men. They circled the stranded schooner for more than two hours, but still there was no sign of life from on board and still no distress signals.

Nor was there any response to calls—only the whistle of the chill and penetrating February winds through the ship's rigging and the roar of the waves on the dread shoals. A boiling surf frothed and spumed like lava spouting from a vexed volcano as the vessel bit deeper into the sand with every curl of a new breaker. Finally the coastguardmen returned to the beach for further instructions. The ownership of the *Carroll M. Deering* was checked in the Marine Register and it was found to be a $200,000 schooner of 2,114 tons built at Bath, Maine, the previous year. Her owners were notified of her plight, and a cutter from Wilmington was dispatched to the scene. Coast guard crews from two other near-by stations were also rushed in to help.

When the rough sea subsided about the shoals, the coastguardmen returned to the amazing ship, still sitting there in her spreading white sails and tugging at the sand that held her bottom fast. The schooner was still intact but now quite high out of the water on the shoals. The sea was comparatively calm. The coastguardmen climbed aboard.

What they found after they scrambled up the side and over the ship's rail was so strange that it is still a favorite topic at the firesides of the people of the coast country. The coastguardmen saw why no distress signals had gone up from the ship as she plowed into the shoals the night before. There was no man on board to send up a signal. She ran ashore because there was no helmsman to guide her. The entire crew of the *Carroll M. Deering* had vanished!

Only one living thing was found as the ship was searched from stem to stern—a lean gray cat; and the only sound not made by sea or creaking timber was the faint and pitiful mewing of the cat, coming from the galley. What a story that cat could have told had she been a modern Puss-in-Boots instead of an ordinary ship's cat!

Most of the ship's papers, charts, and nautical instruments were missing. The steering apparatus was smashed, apparently by a sledge hammer that was propped casually against the wheel. The rudder swung free, allowing the vessel to drift with the current. The ship's stores, signal flags, and gear were stowed intact. The bunks were all made up, a meal was cooked, the tables set, and food—only partly consumed—was left on the plates. Other food was in the pots on the icy-cold stove. Everything was shipshape and there was no evidence of violence. Lights still burned in the ship's salon.

While the men on board pondered the strange case of the wandering, crewless schooner, the coast guard on shore was getting information to piece together the events of the *Carroll M. Deering's* last cruise. In August, six months before, the schooner had cleared Newport News, Virginia, with a cargo of coal, bound for Rio de Janeiro by way of Lewes, Delaware, under the command of Captain William Merritt of Portland, Maine. Merritt's son was first mate. The vessel was but a few days underway when Captain Merritt was taken sick; so she put in at the Delaware Breakwater, at Lewes,—and Captain Merritt was transferred from the ship to a hospital. His son went with him. There was some suggestion in subsequent investigations that Captain Merritt had been having trouble with the crew, which had been signed on at Norfolk, and pleaded ill health as an excuse to leave the ship.

At any rate, a new master and first mate came aboard. The captain who took over at Lewes was William B. Wormell of Boston, a hardy but likable skipper who had weathered roaring typhoons in the China Sea and defied the furies of the

North Atlantic in every type of windjammer that floated. He came down from New York and brought a trusted and competent first mate with him. This delay was such that it was early September before the *Deering* proceeded on its run to Rio. After a comparatively calm trip, she tied up at the South American port and discharged her cargo of coal. Since there was nothing scheduled to transport back to the United States, she cleared Rio de Janeiro "light" on December 3. On the trip home she called at Barbados, where Captain Wormell found orders awaiting him to proceed without cargo to Norfolk. While at Barbados, Captain Wormell complained to his ship's agents at Bridgetown, Barbados, of the unruliness of the crew and mentioned his own ill health.

The crew, in addition to the American mate, consisted of a Finnish boatswain, a Negro steward, and six Danish sailors. Cafe loungers at Barbados were reported to have overheard a heated argument in which the mate of the *Deering* threatened to "get the old man" before the vessel reached Norfolk, referring presumably to Captain Wormell.

On January 9, 1921, when the *Deering* left Barbados in her backwash, she had cleared a port for the last time. At 2:00 P.M. on January 23, she passed the Cape Fear lightship, off the lower North Carolina coast. Then, six days later, she passed the Cape Lookout lightship off Diamond Shoals. The distance between these two lightships is only eighty miles. The *Deering* was six days in sailing that distance.

The captain of the Cape Lookout lightship reported later that when the *Deering* passed him a man stood on the deck and hailed him through a megaphone, notifying him that the *Deering* had lost her anchors in a storm when coming up the the coast, and asked that boats watch for her as she approached

Norfolk. When the captain of the Cape Lookout lightship testified at later hearings, his description of the man who signaled him from the deck of the *Deering* did not tally with the appearance of Captain Wormell. The lightship captain said, too, that the man did not look or act like a ship's officer. Also, he added, crewmen were scattered about the ship in such a way as to indicate lack of discipline.

Back on the *Deering,* stuck fast on the shoals, a fine-toothed-comb search was being made through the cabin, forecastle head, steerage, and holds. Little was found to throw light on what happened aboard the ship during the last hours before she was beached. But there ensued one of the most exhaustive investigations in maritime records—so exhaustive, in fact, that before it ended, six government departments besides the coast guard became involved: the Navy and the Justice, Treasury, State, Navigation, and Commerce departments.

The strange vessel was salvaged, and all her usable sails, furniture, and other gear were sold at public auction. Wreckers then left the *Carroll M. Deering* to the mercy of the wind and waves. The elements started their grim business of gnawing her into nothingness. The stranded vessel began to go to pieces there off Hatteras on March 21. The stern beached about twelve miles from the cape. This wreckage consisted of a poop deck, counter, port side, deck house, and after house. Hundreds of sea gulls chose this wreckage for a roost and scores of them built nests there. The nights were made hideous with their shrill cries. There was talk of spirits walking the boards of the *Carroll M. Deering,* and the presence of this remnant of the mystery ship soon became a nightmare to the natives of the beach near by. Finally they appealed to the government. United States Coast Guard Headquarters ordered that the *Carroll M. Deering's* remains be blown up. But this order was destined never to be carried out; while the coast guard cutters at Norfolk made ready to put out to sea with dynamite to blow up the stranded piece of wreckage, a sudden storm came up and within a few hours a howling northeast gale was piling the sea up high on the beach at Hatteras. Tremendous waves hit the derelict ghost ship, and she groaned and whined under their terrific beating. Soon her timbers began to loosen and she went to pieces rapidly.

The next day, when the wind was no more than a breeze and the sea was smooth and oily, hundreds of birds, made homeless by the blow that disintegrated their wreck, circled and recircled the spot, screeching and crying. Some said these noises were the cries of departed spirits hovering over the scattered remains of the schooner. All that remained of the ghost ship was timber scattered for miles along the beach.

It has been many years since some grim spectre took over the wheel of the trim and sturdy *Carroll M. Deering* and veered the crewless vessel off her course into a port of doom. As the seasons have come and gone, innumerable theories about the *Deering* and her fate have been propounded—each as plausible as another and each as absurd. But throughout the investigations, and in all the years since, no theory has been overlooked and no angle scoffed at. No possible clue has been thought insignificant. Yet the deeper the probe the deeper the mystery of the missing crew.

When first news of the mysterious schooner was flashed over the world, a young woman in Boston, Miss Lulu Wormell, daughter of the ship's Captain William B. Wormell, said she was positive that the ship had fallen into the hands of twentieth-century pirates and that her father and his crew and been murdered at sea. In subsequent investigations she made out a pretty good case.

On the chart that was salvaged from the ship, Miss Wormell said she could identify her father's handwriting up to January 23, the day the ship passed the Cape Fear lightship, and that after that the entries were made by a different hand. It was six days after January 23 that the captain of the Cape Lookout lightship said the *Deering* passed his ship and that he was hailed by the man on deck who did not look or act like a ship's officer.

The captain of the Cape Lookout lightship also testified that a steamer passed his station shortly after the *Deering* and refused to stop when he flagged an international code signal, "Have important message." He stated that he then blew his No. 12 chime whistle which could be heard for five miles; contrary to the unwritten law of the high seas, the steamer still refused to stop. The lightship captain said he wanted to notify the steamer that the *Deering* had lost her anchors.

The most important evidence against the modern buccaneering theory is that the ship carried no valuables, not even a cargo. It seems unreasonable that pirates would have risked their necks simply for the personal belongings of a ship's crew. Besides, there was no evidence of a topsy-turvy search of the ship for things of value. A note found in a floating bottle, indicating that the *Deering* had indeed been the victim of pirates, was produced but was later proved to be a fraud.

Other theories included that of a mass suicide at sea, with a suggested possibility that the crew had contracted some dread tropical disease and that the men had sacrificed their lives to prevent a fatal epidemic in the States. But such a theory would contemplate finding bodies and did not explain the missing lifeboats.

Also suggested, perhaps by the indication of mutiny that came from the reportedly overheard conversation at Barbados, was the possibility that the crew murdered the captain, set the ship adrift, landed in the open boats and burned them on some beach. But many who had sailed with Captain Wormell said he was a sociable individual and highly popular with his subordinates.

Then there is the theory—perhaps the most plausible of all—that the crew abandoned the ship in lifeboats for some reason and were picked up by the steamer *Hewitt,* known to have been at a position near the *Deering* at the time. The *Hewitt* was carrying a cargo of sulphur to New York. A few days after the *Deering* went aground there was a great flash of fire off the New Jersey coast and high billows of smoke hung in the air. The *Hewitt* never reached New York and it became evident that her cargo had exploded. Perhaps both crews, then aboard, were lost—perhaps.

The *Deering* investigation was finally brought to a close with the terse statement of one of the federal government officials. He said, "We might just as well have searched a painted ship on a painted ocean for sight of the vanished crew." What happened aboard the ship from the time she cleared a South American port until she put in at Hatteras, a ghost ship in full sail without captain or crew, will never be known.

Meanwhile the *Carroll M. Deering,* which once swept down the ocean highways with her snow-white canvas towering away to the royal yards, and which once surged bravely through the raging gales and biting blasts of ill-tempered seas, has finally broken up and rotted away in the death clutches of a treacherous sand bar—taking with her into oblivion one of the most baffling secrets of the ocean that washes our Carolina coast.

The Mysterious Death of Beautiful Nell Cropsey

THERE is a jingle of a song that's popular with school-boys—and others—about one of our eastern North Carolina rivers. It says something about how "way down on the Pasquotank the bullfrogs jump from bank to bank." Well, the bullfrogs do nothing of the kind, of course. Bullfrogs along the banks of the Pasquotank would need rocket attachments on their jumping equipment to get even part way across the Pasquotank in a jump.

The big, sprawling, flat, sluggish stream spreads out in the Elizabeth City vicinity to make a picturesque world of water, cypress trees, and flat low country. It's a great boating place,

a fine fishing ground, and—for purposes of giving this particular story a backdrop—a beautiful setting for romantic
lovers who thrive best on combinations of lapping water, full
moon, and overhanging trees.

Into this sort of world the Cropsey family moved in 1898.
They came from New York State, and the family consisted of
parents and several young daughters. W. H. Cropsey, head
of the house, was a buyer of potatoes and grain for a New
York commission merchant, and the family had been living
in Brooklyn.

The Cropseys liked the Pasquotank River country, and that
section liked them. In spite of being a Yankee and having to
face some little prejudice on that score, Mr. Cropsey succeeded
at once, both financially and socially, in what was then a little
coastal town. He established his family in a fine home two
hundred feet from the bank of the Pasquotank River in the
best residential section of the community of that day. This
home was often the scene of gay parties.

All of the daughters were pretty, and two were of marriage-
able age when the family arrived in Elizabeth City. These
were Ollie, eighteen, and Nellie, a year and a half younger.
And you may be sure that the young blades of the community
found ways and means of being presented to the Misses
Cropsey.

Reports from that day indicate that Nellie was exquisitely
beautiful indeed—a young woman of the kind that artists
dream of finding and lovers always see through mist-clouded
eyes. Through the turbulent times that came to the Cropseys,
one adjective became so affixed to Nellie's name and so much
a part of her as a young lady that she has always been referred
to as "Beautiful Nell" Cropsey. That the adjective was not

mere legend, but was well deserved, may be seen in a life-size head-and-shoulder photograph of Beautiful Nell that is still in existence. It is done in color and shows, as well as a photograph can, dark blue eyes glowing with mischief and intelligence, chestnut-brown hair, a finely shaped mouth, a delicately pointed nose, and a high forehead that lends dignity to the face of the young woman.

Back at the turn of the present century one of Beautiful Nell Cropsey's suitors was James Wilcox, twenty-five years of age and the son of Thomas P. Wilcox, a former sheriff of Pasquotank County. He became interested in Beautiful Nell soon after the family came south to Elizabeth City and he gave her his attention for some three years. During this time he was working as a lumber-mill hand and taking a correspondence-school law course.

On Wednesday night, November 20, 1901, Jim Wilcox was calling on Beautiful Nell Cropsey, as was his custom. But their love affair was not going smoothly. Nellie had apparently been thinking of their three-year courtship, which had as yet brought no marriage proposal. Not being willing to wait forever, she had thought that by igniting a spark of jealousy— by showing her suitor that she was attractive to other men— she could prompt a certain question.

So Nellie had been engaging in mild flirtations, and Jim had been sulking. Then there was a quarrel, which ended with Nellie's tears and Jim's apologies. Because of this turn of affairs, members of the family said, Jim Wilcox was silent and morose on that particular night in November. He did not, in fact, speak for a good part of the evening.

Ollie Cropsey, Nellie's sister, was there that evening, as was the girls' cousin, Carrie Cropsey, from New York, and Roy

Crawford, an office clerk who had been paying considerable attention to Ollie. As the young people sat talking, the conversation turned to—of all things—suicide and its methods.

"I'd rather drown myself," Jim Wilcox announced.

"Oh, I wouldn't! I'd rather freeze to death," Nellie said gaily.

Ollie said later that Jim, who wasn't talking much, kept watching the clock. Finally at 11:00 P.M. he rose and said he had to go.

According to Ollie's story, Jim held the front door open a crack as he went out and whispered back through the narrow opening to Nellie that he wanted to speak to her. Nellie looked questioningly at Ollie, who later said she indicated with a nod that her sister should talk to Jim Wilcox. So Nell stepped out on the front porch of her home with her sweetheart.

And in stepping across the threshold of her home and out into the chill night air of late fall, Beautiful Nell Cropsey stepped, it seems, into another world, never to be seen alive again. This mystery has fascinated the people of North Carolina, particularly in the East Coast country, for nearly half a century.

Ollie Cropsey said later that after her sister stepped out on the porch with Jim Wilcox she heard a quick snap or thump as if someone had bumped suddenly into the door.

In the later gathering together of loose ends of information Caleb Parker reported that he drove by the Cropsey home in his buggy at about 11:00 P.M. and that he saw Jim and Nell standing at the gate to the Cropsey yard, in the moonlight. Jim had his arm around Nell and her head was bowed, Caleb said.

Meantime, inside the Cropsey home, Cousin Carrie went

upstairs for the night. Then Sister Ollie's caller, Roy Crawford, took his leave. He said he saw no one out in front as he
swung off the porch and down the street. When 11:45 came
and Nell had not come back into the house, Ollie went to the
front hall and found the door standing wide open to the
night air. The screen door was pushed so far back that it had
broken the spring. Ollie called her sister but received no reply.
Puzzled, she closed the door and went upstairs.

Ollie said she decided that Nellie had perhaps already come
in and gone to her room silently so as not to disturb the others.
Ollie felt her sister's bed in the dark, but found it empty. In
connection with her description of a growing fear, given
later, Ollie recalled that a strange bright light from the moon
came in at her bedroom window.

The clock struck twelve. She drowsed, but was quickly
pulled back to consciousness by the whistle of a distant lumber
mill. And then bedlam broke loose in the Cropsey back
yard. The Cropsey dogs began to bark and the pigs to squeal.
A neighbor shouted: "Cropsey! Cropsey! Someone's after
your pigs! Get your gun!"

Ollie jumped up and ran from her room into the hallway,
calling to her father not to shoot. "Nell and Jim are outside
somewhere." Mr. Cropsey pulled on his pants over his nightshirt, stuck his feet into a pair of shoes, and paddled down the
stairs with his rifle in his hands. Pig theft, or his daughter and
her beau wandering around the grounds—either prospect
irritated him.

Ollie said that he grumbled: "What's that girl thinking of,
out at this hour disturbing the dogs and the pigs!"

But the father, ready to give the young people a piece of
his mind, did not find Nell, Jim—or a thief. He returned to

the house to see if Nell had gone to bed without her sister's knowledge. She was not to be found, and their uneasiness increased.

The father, now thoroughly aroused, set out for the Wilcox home. Striding up to the Wilcox porch after a ten-minute walk through the night, Cropsey pounded on the door. The drowsy ex-sheriff answered his knocking and Cropsey explained his mission and expressed his displeasure with young Wilcox.

"Why, Jim's been home since midnight. He's fast asleep," protested the elder Wilcox.

Jim was called and in a few minutes he appeared in his nightshirt, apparently just awakened from a sound sleep.

"Where's Nell?" Cropsey demanded.

"Nellie?" Jim asked in surprise. "Why, home, isn't she? I left her on your front porch around 11:15."

By this time anger had given way to fear, and the worried father hastened to the near-by home of Police Chief Henry Dawson to report the girl's disappearance. Dawson dressed and accompanied Cropsey back to his home. Together the two men searched the house and grounds. They looked all about the rustic summerhouse down at the river's edge and the boat-landing. They searched the neighbors' yards. But there was no Nell.

They went back to the Wilcox home to demand from Jim an exact account of the events of the evening.

Jim gave this step-by-step version. He said that he left his own home at 8:00 P.M. to take Nell Cropsey an umbrella that he had borrowed and to return a picture of her that she had given him two years before. He said that he had decided to return the items and not see the young woman again. He had not planned to stay for the evening.

But Ollie answered the door and he had to go in and wait for Nell to come downstairs. The evening wore on and it was eleven o'clock before he asked Nell to go to the front porch with him. There, he said, he gave her the picture and the umbrella and told her that he wasn't coming back again.

"What did she say?" Chief Dawson demanded.

"She began to cry," Jim said. "She leaned against a porch post with her head on her arm. I told her she had better go in, but she wouldn't stop crying. After about ten minutes I told her I had to meet a man at Barnes' barroom before it closed and had to leave. She stopped crying long enough to say, 'Well, go on then!' So I did go."

Wilcox said that he was much agitated and wandered about in the moonlight for a few minutes—maybe half an hour— and then went to Barnes' bar, had a glass of beer with Len Owens and went home to bed.

Chief Dawson checked and found the umbrella in the hall-rack at the Cropsey home, but the picture was not to be found. He decided that he would detain Wilcox until the case was cleared up, and before the dawn of November 21, the young man was behind the bars of Pasquotank jail, in charge of Deputy Sheriff Charles Reid.

The next day brought no trace of the girl. Bloodhounds followed her trail from the porch to the rustic house, and then to the boathouse. But there was no other sign that she had been to either place. The river was dragged over a wide area and more than one hundred houses were searched in the town and adjoining county. But Nell had vanished. Feeling ran high against Jim Wilcox, who was now formally charged with abduction.

And then came silence and mystery and suspense—hours, days, and weeks of it. And with it all, absolutely no trace of Beautiful Nell Cropsey, who had stepped out of her front door and vanished.

In that period Jim Wilcox was of course questioned again and again. Evidence developed tending to show that although he left the Cropsey home at eleven, he did not reach his own home until one o'clock the next morning. A witness also reported that Wilcox had a blackjack, which he boastfully showed to acquaintances.

As news of the disappearance spread, the Cropsey family received notes from people all over the state, who reported that they had seen Beautiful Nell, now known generally by that descriptive title, in this city and that city.

Ollie recalled that Nell had told her of a terrible dream she had a few nights before the disappearance, a dream so horrible that it made Nell feel that something was going to happen to her. Remembrance of this dream brought no comfort to the distraught family.

On December 24, Mr. Cropsey received an anonymous letter postmarked "Utica, N. Y." The writer said that he had information concerning events of the night of November 20. He said Jim Wilcox left Nellie Cropsey crying on the porch. She was there for some time. (Where she was when Roy Crawford departed, the writer didn't say.) Then the Cropsey dogs barked. Nellie went from the porch into the yard to investigate the cause of the commotion. She found an Elizabeth City man stealing a pig. She recognized him and threatened to tell her father.

Thereupon, the letter continued, this man stunned Nell with a stick, carried her body to the river, dumped it into a boat, and rowed away with her, unconscious or dead.

The writer of the letter predicted that the body of Beautiful Nell would be found at a given spot. He marked that spot on an appended diagram. Cropsey read the letter and noted its contents. If he turned it over to the police, no official notice was taken of it.

And yet, just five days later, Nellie's body was found near the spot marked on the mysterious chart, 150 yards downstream from the Cropsey boathouse.

Every night the heartbroken mother had been going down to the banks of the Pasquotank, which takes on a bay-like shape near the Cropsey home, there to look for her daughter— to search through the night when sleep would not come to her.

This had gone on for days without a whisper of news of Beautiful Nell—days when the family hoped against hope that she was still alive.

And then, on one of her lonely night vigils, Mrs. Cropsey saw something white floating on the water. At her direction and insistence a fisherman rowed out and found the body of Beautiful Nell Cropsey.

A lynching party was quickly formed, but James Wilcox was saved from the wrath of this mob by the Cropseys themselves, according to the word of the county sheriff of the time. The mob came to the jail where Wilcox had been lodged, bringing a rope and screaming that they would swing him from the nearest tree. Mr. Cropsey, the father, backed by Mrs. Cropsey, refused to have anything to do with the mob.

In the tremendous excitement that gripped the Elizabeth City area, loud and persistent threats of lynching continued.

Finally Sheriff Grandy wired Governor Charles B. Aycock for the assistance of "naval reserves"—a part of the State Guard. The reserve group was ordered to the jail, and with this arrival of the military the crowds of angered citizens ceased to gather.

Some stray bits of evidence, all entirely circumstantial, began to point a rather wavering finger at Jim Wilcox. In addition to the unexplained period of time on the night that Beautiful Nell disappeared, the blackjack he carried, and the suggested motive that he was about to be jilted by a pretty girl, it was recalled that on the Saturday before the disappearance of Nellie Cropsey, Jim Wilcox had tried to get her to go sailing with him on the Pasquotank. Both Nell and her sister Ollie were afraid of the venture and the invitation was refused.

And when Wilcox did get Cousin Carrie and another of the Cropsey sisters to go out with him in his boat, he didn't bring them back until 6:00 P.M., which was dark at that time of year. Everybody was uneasy until they finally put in appearance. And just before he returned to the house with the girls, young Wilcox suggested wrapping the sister in a blanket and bring her in as if she were dead, just to frighten the mother.

The coroner, Irving Fearing, and two Elizabeth City physicians found that the young Cropsey woman had come to her death "by being stricken a blow on the left temple and by being drowned in the Pasquotank river." This rather curious statement excited argument among medical men for months to follow. But contrary to the usual condition after death by drowning, the coroner's report stated that no water was found in the lungs of the dead girl. The blow on the temple, the two physicians agreed, had been struck by a round, padded instrument, something like a blackjack. There were no other marks of violence.

All this assortment of circumstances seemed to add up to enough evidence for the authorities to take James Wilcox to trial, faced with a charge of murder. As the trial finally got underway, two hundred talesmen were called and the selection of a jury was a long and tedious undertaking. When twelve men were finally seated in the jury box, Solicitor George W. Ward told them that he could show by motive and opportunity that Wilcox killed Nellie Cropsey; that the young man was tired of the girl but feared that if he threw her over after three years of courtship, she would provoke a public scandal. Anticipating the defense, the prosecutor scoffed at the idea that "a healthy, happy girl" would kill herself. As the trial unfolded, Ward sought to show, through medical testimony, that Nellie did not die of drowning, that she was dying or dead before being put into the river. Even the coroner, whose report originally said that she had drowned, ended by testifying that she had not.

The prosecution based its case largely on the fact that Wilcox was the last man to see Beautiful Nell Cropsey alive. In the prolonged and sensation-packed trial he was convicted and sentenced to death. Eventually a new trial was granted and was given to him in another county, where he was again convicted—this time for second-degree murder. A prison sentence followed. In neither trial did Wilcox take the stand in his own defense to deny the crime with his own lips.

Wilcox served behind prison bars of the state prison until December 20, 1920, when he was pardoned by Governor Thomas W. Bickett. Previously Governor Locke Craig had twice refused to pardon the man, and Governor Bickett refused a pardon once, before he finally granted favorable action. Neither of the governors could apparently understand why Wilcox had not taken the stand to deny his guilt and offer a defense for himself.

In setting Wilcox free from prison Governor Bickett seems to have become convinced that Wilcox had not killed his sweetheart as charged.

Roland F. Beasley, a veteran newspaper man of Monroe and Charlotte, believes that Governor Bickett discovered the true explanation of the death of Nell Cropsey. Editor Beasley once said, "I think that Jim Wilcox told Governor Bickett the truth about what happened that night in 1901 and that Governor Bickett believed him, and for that reason pardoned him."

No one knows what Wilcox told Governor Bickett, and no one ever will know, for both men are dead. Mr. Beasley said that Governor Bickett told him, some weeks before he pardoned Wilcox, that there was an explanation in the case compatible with Wilcox's innocence. The Governor added that he was to be at a prison camp in the mountains where Wilcox was confined, and planned to talk with the prisoner. "If he says what I think he probably will say, I expect to pardon him," Editor Beasley quoted Governor Bickett as saying.

The conversation did take place between the Governor and the prisoner. What was said has never been revealed and has never been placed in any record. But Jim Wilcox went home.

Editor Beasley happened to be on a train going to Elizabeth City on Christmas Eve, December 24, 1920, and Jim Wilcox was on that same train, going home from prison. Editor Beasley didn't know Wilcox was on the train until it stopped at

Elizabeth City and Wilcox got off, dressed like a mountain climber with a squirrel tail in his hat-band and two dogs on chains. He presented a picture quite different from that of the dapper young lover of eighteen years before, on trial for his life.

After his release from prison he lived as a recluse. He felt as if everyone wanted to shun him. "People don't want me around," he once said.

And then, after a score of years had passed, the story took a new turn. Jim Wilcox shot his own head off with a shotgun.

At that time, when a new generation was reading the newspapers, it was just another suicide. But to those who had followed the case back in 1901, it was another startling chapter in the story of the strange death of Beautiful Nell Cropsey. After fifty years it is still an unsolved mystery.

A Treasure Ship off Wrightsville

THAT fascinating stretch of ocean front that extends from Topsail Inlet, on the North Carolina coast to Georgetown, in South Carolina, is the unmarked grave of a strange squadron of ships that sailed the seas and fought for the Southern Confederacy.

When the War between the States broke out in the early sixties, the Confederacy didn't have a ship—not one! North Carolina's contribution to the hastily improvised navy was an old tugboat and a small passenger vessel, both unfit for sea service. But this state also contributed a group of men who helped to make a navy for the Confederacy—such a navy as had never been seen or heard of before.

Of course, as the war years wore on, the South got her sea legs—and fast. A Confederacy, once without a navy, soon threatened to drive the merchant flag of the United States from the Atlantic Ocean. In fact, it was the Confederacy that came forward with a droll but dynamic iron battering ram that floated, and in so doing revolutionized the navies of the world. The *Merrimac,* an ironclad sea monster, brought a new potency to warfare at sea.

The most perfect military or naval blockade in modern history is credited to the Yankee forces during America's War between the States, when the United States Navy finally threw a complete barricade around leading Southern ports. In that war the South possessed a long land frontier, but except along the Mexican border it was dominated by the United States forces. The Federal Navy held several bases in Southern territory, and commerce with foreign ports became a great Confederate problem during the final phases of the war.

To meet this situation, the Confederate states brought into use a new ship built for a new purpose—the blockade runner. Today remains of these ships lie buried along our coast by the score, some visible and some covered by the sea that bred the men who devised and manned this strange craft.

Especially built and especially equipped for the job that was at hand, these blockade runners were fast for their day, shallow of draft, silent, small, and powerful. They were intended for use in slipping quietly through the Federal blockade lines under cover of darkness to go to foreign ports and bring back to the South the food, the clothing, the medicine, the arms and the ammunition needed to carry on the war.

It was this new and strange and brave fleet that kept the Confederacy alive long after it would otherwise have collapsed in surrender. Slipping into and out of inlets on the North Carolina coast, daring crews on dangerous missions kept the life-giving supply route open and provided the substance that kept that thin gray line of men called the Army of Northern Virginia from starving and sustained the Lost Cause for months after it was indeed lost.

These compact aquatic life-savers were sidewheel steamers of between 400 and 700 tons gross, were rigged as fore-and-aft schooners, and had from one to three funnels. They were 200 feet long and drew from 5 to 11 feet of water. They could make 16 knots as a top speed (which would be 19 miles an hour if the speed were figured for a land vehicle).

By the winter of 1862, the Confederacy had developed this new technique for importing the badly needed supplies of war. And blockade running was an extra-hazardous business. The blockade runner could use smaller inlets, less carefully watched by the enemy, where many of the channels were known only to the local harbor pilots, who had in most instances ended up aboard a blockade runner.

Summer visitors to points along the beaches from Topsail Inlet south can still see the battered hulls of some of the most beautiful ships of the War between the States rearing out of the ocean at low tide. Each barnacle-clad derelict represents an amazing page in the South's famous—and unique—fight of the sixties. These slumbering rusted ghosts were once proud and fiery sidewheelers that took their turn at running the Federal gauntlet with the best of them. Mute tragedy still pervades these spots, as the curling swells lick the wounds of the old ghost ships.

And unless these ghosts are moved, they will be there, snuggled against the white corrugated ocean bottom, for centuries to come. They were made of thick, rugged iron, which does not corrode like steel in salt water.

One such ghost is visible today, at low tide, off Wrightsville Beach. Thousands of summer beach visitors who have made merry at the Lumina dance pavilion and entertainment center have seen these black remains of a gallant blockade runner —today a battered lump of iron and junk plainly visible at low tide. The ancient piece of wreckage is just three hundred yards off the southeast corner of Lumina.

This motley thing, against which the waves wash unceasingly, is the remains of the *Fanny and Jennie*, one of the Confederate blockade runners. The barnacle-clad hulk is all that remains of a sleek and daring vessel once manned by youthful North Carolina sailors who knew the danger that went with each try at a slip through the line of enemy ships, and who offered their lives with each sailing.

In addition to the sentiment that surrounds the rusting innards of an already wasted hull, this particular wreck also supports a story of a lost treasure—a treasure that has never been found, although it rests so near a summer playground where thousands gather each year. The old derelict has been gradually wearing away for eighty-two years, but she may still hold fast to a special part of a cargo she was bringing from an English port to aid Confederate soldiers and bolster the Lost Cause, a valuable memento to be delivered to General Robert E. Lee.

To tell the story of the *Fanny and Jennie* derelict, we must go back to the night of February 9, 1864. A murky gloom along the North Carolina coast provided a proper setting for what took place. Our fore-and-aft sidewheeler, built by the famous Clyde shipbuilders, was riding the rough sea off the coast with all the grace of a feather. The long, narrow ship, built especially for blockade running, slipped along like a shadow.

She was almost brand new then, was the *Fanny and Jennie*. She had been put into this new service only a short time before. And she was a queen of the blockade running fleet. She was just getting used to the salty tang of the sea.

The *Fanny and Jennie* was out of Bermuda on this February night as she plowed the lead-colored sea headed for New Inlet and Wilmington, bringing in war contraband. The ship had reached a position off Moore's Inlet—or Wrightsville Beach—and was edging in cautiously to avoid the enemy craft that patrolled these waters closely.

Out of the blackness of that night suddenly came the boom of a voice ordering that the *Fanny and Jennie* "Heave to."

The captain and the pilot, at the pilot house, heard the order. But the captain's answer was not sent back across the waves; instead it was shouted into the speaking tube of his own ship. He filled the engine room with: "Enemy astern. Give us all the pressure you can. Full speed ahead."

And the half-naked stokers, streaked with the black of coal dust, heard this order through the dim light in which they worked, and the furnace doors swung open to receive shovel after shovel of coal into the red-hot, yawning mouths of the fire boxes.

The *Fanny and Jennie* must have fairly lunged forward as she started a zig-zag course like a water bug on a lily pond. Darting from port to starboard, she began the race that every man aboard knew was one of life or death for ship and crew.

"Heave to or I'll blow you out of the water," came back from a point out there in the blackness, dangerously near. And the order was quickly followed by a red stab of fire in the dark, a reverberant boom, a whine, and a splash beyond the Confederate ship. The shot was purposely high, but the Dixie runner only strove for more speed and leaped forward in the blackness, slicing the water as her side-wheels strained against the resisting ocean.

Then there was another flash from the void of night, this time from another direction. And those who manned the *Fanny and Jennie* knew that another blockader was on her heels.

After those two sampling shots, the two blockaders, hardly more than two hundred yards from the *Fanny and Jennie*, began to get a range and opened fire with all guns belching away in a great fury to deliver grape, canister, and shrapnel on and around the *Fanny and Jennie*. The Yankee guns spattered the blockade runner with this deadly hail. For minutes that must have seemed like hours these murderous blasts continued. Powder fumes filled the wind, and the crack of cannon split the night.

The captain of the *Fanny and Jennie,* a sage of the Cape Fear waters and a veteran of many runs through the blockade, had by now located the enemy ships to his stern and on his port side. He decided to head for shore. On a ship that drew only eight feet of water, he had some hope and assurance that he could make the inlet.

And then a soaring burst of fire caught the gallant *Fanny and Jennie* amidship, rocking her from stem to stern and causing her to leap from the water. Quivering convulsively, she sloshed back minus a paddle wheel and a foremast. Her smokestacks rolled aimlessly on the deck. Tons of water poured in through a jagged hole in her waterline.

The engines faltered, the vibrations of the pulsing, racing ocean greyhound stopped, and the *Fanny and Jennie* slowed down to a glide through the water. But still the cannons of the two blockaders continued to pound the runner with red explosions and heavy thuds.

The beach was just ahead. All surviving hands rushed to the boats. The enemy, because of shoal water, fired a final volley and then dropped back to watch. The once sleek Clyde-built runner, her hold full of water, her cargo ruined, and her entire structure blasted by the enemy cannon fire, bumped along the ocean bottom, slumped over on her side, swung half-way around, and slowly sank to a final rest in the surf.

And there the *Fanny and Jennie* has been for nearly a century, subjected all this time to the incessant pounding of the sea.

All hands reached shore safely. But the captain, remembering something that had been trusted to his care and safekeeping for ultimate delivery, started back to the wreck. His purser went with him. The boat in which they made this impulsive return trip was capsized by belligerent waves and both men were drowned.

The story has it that only the captain and the purser knew about the object they went back for. But it was later revealed that aboard the *Fanny and Jennie* was a solid gold, jewel-studded sword bearing this inscription: "To General Robert E. Lee, From his British Sympathisers." There is no record of the sword's ever having been recovered.

There is also a tradition that the ship had—in addition to the sword, which would in itself be worth a king's ransom today—other treasures in its cargo, besides the food and clothing that were supposed to find their way inland and to the battlefields of Virginia. These hints suggest gold, coming from the people of foreign shores who had sympathy for the South. The treasure was to have been used in further prosecution of the war for the Confederacy.

At this very moment the sea is pounding the remains of the *Fanny and Jennie* just off Wrightsville Beach, close in to the Lumina pavilion. The tides of more than eighty years have washed over the old derelict. And somewhere under the curling swells of the Atlantic, a golden sword from English admirers may lie, intended for Robert E. Lee.

The Vanishing of Peter Dromgoole

~~~~~~

CHAPEL HILL is unlike any other spot under the Carolina sun, or, for that matter, under the Carolina moon of song and story. Chapel Hill is—well, just Chapel Hill. Having said that, you have given a complete travelog to the person who has been there for a casual visit or a week-end, or who has had the privilege of four years in the state's University.

Chapel Hill is an old place and at the same time an attractive place, as so often happens. It has its traditions, its history, its stories, its romantic and interesting yesterday as well as its dynamic and throbbing today.

Here is a story with which every freshman becomes familiar

shortly after entering the University. Without it no collection of North Carolina mysteries, legends, or tales would be complete.

It is a story of passion, of courage, of love, of bloodshed, and it savors of other lands and other ages, when heart-torn lovers settled differences at dawn with pistol or blade.

The locale of the story is now marked by a recent-year construction of a castle that duplicates the strongholds of pre-Norman England. The castle stands on Piney Prospect, just east of Chapel Hill proper. There, above a purple-misted valley, the strange end of one Peter Dromgoole is said to have occurred. The story is as quaint as the castle that stands today on the brow of the hill.

Dromgoole rock is there, a huge boulder with reddish discolorations, close beside Hippol Castle of the Gimghoul lodge, generally referred to as Gimghoul Castle. This rock is of absorbing interest, for it is supposed to cover the hurried grave of Peter Dromgoole. Hovering over the mottled rock is the romantic legend that the red stains on it are the blood of Peter Dromgoole. The rains, the frosts, and the snows of a century have never erased the dark red splotches. At the possible expense of our story, let it be said in the interest of science, if not of mystery, that members of the University Geology Department consider the red splotches to be rust stains coming from the metallic content of the stone.

There are several versions of the Dromgoole story. It has been incorporated into the plots of at least two novels and is the theme of one poem. But what appears to be the most authentic version was written by a member of the Dromgoole family after exhaustive research and a thorough reading of dozens of letters and documents found hidden away in the old Dromgoole homestead in Brunswick County, Virginia. Three letters, written by young Peter Dromgoole during his student days at the University of North Carolina, throw some light on the mystery. The most plausible version, as worked out by Peter's kinsman is this:

Peter Dromgoole, son of a prominent Virginia family, entered the University of North Carolina in the year 1831. There is some evidence that Peter was reckless and unsteady, fond of card playing and wild company. In accordance with the ways of students at Chapel Hill and college students everywhere, he fell in love. He fell desperately in love. It was before the day of co-eds, and the object of this great affection was a young woman who lived in the University community.

Like all lovers at Chapel Hill, in every college generation since William R. Davie sat astride a horse and picked the site for the first University building, Peter Dromgoole naturally selected Piney Prospect as a favorite trysting place. Sitting close on the fern-bordered precipice, looking down into the valley below (between looks into each other's eyes), these sweethearts loitered and whispered their love. Piney Prospect has heard much of hopes and expectations and plans and anticipations in its day.

Peter's sweetheart was named Fanny. A spring at the base of the Piney Prospect plateau was one of the favorite spots of the lovers. This spring still exists, still bubbles forth water, and is today known as Miss Fanny's Spring.

But a shadow came to cloud the horizon for Peter Dromgoole and the light of his life. There was another who also adored the pretty Chapel Hill girl. He had been rejected in favor of the young Virginian. And as the weeks saw interest grow into gentle affection and affection develop into love, the rejected suitor became insanely jealous of Peter Dromgoole. There was a challenge to a duel, in keeping with a gentleman's way of settling things in that day. Peter Dromgoole accepted the challenge, of course. Seconds were chosen. And on a certain night when the moon was high and shone down full on Piney Prospect, the contenders met there and the members of the little party stepped off the distance.

There was a signal and pistols flashed. Peter Dromgoole swayed and fell. Blood oozed from a wound in his chest. His second said that as he lay there he cried out that it is terrible to die when life is young and hopes are bright. And, as death hastened, he called the names of his mother and his sweetheart. The girl that he won in life on beautiful Piney Prospect he lost in death at the same spot.

The young students who remained there under the moon lifted the dying young man tenderly and placed him on the gently-rounded top of a great boulder. And it was there that he died. The boys who participated in the dueling party were terrified in the presence of the lifeless form. Only then did they begin to realize the full seriousness of their plight. They held a hurried whispered conference out there in the night and pledged themselves to eternal secrecy. The surviving rival and the two seconds then secured tools and buried their newly-dead friend and fellow student under the big rock, reddened with his still-warm blood. And when dawn was streaking through the trees, the three students returned to their dormitory with leaden hearts.

The next day, Peter's sweetheart went to the trysting place, but no lover appeared. And in the days that followed she went back there time after time, always hopeful but always to be disappointed. She made discreet inquiries after the young man, but the only general knowledge was that he had disappeared from the University campus.

So the young lady continued to watch and wonder and wait at intervals close beside the big rock. There she wept silently and unknowingly beside the tomb of her lover.

The mysterious disappearance of Peter Dromgoole sapped the young lady's life; and, according to the story, she grew silent and seemed to live in a trance. Finally, too weak and ill to make her pilgrimage to Piney Prospect, she sat at a window in her home and waited for the lover who could not return. In perfectly good story-book fashion, Peter's sweetheart died of a broken heart.

This particular version fills in some background between the known facts in the life of Peter Dromgoole at Chapel Hill and his mysterious disappearance from the campus of the University of North Carolina back in the 1830's.

There is another version of the duel story which has it that Peter Dromgoole, who was rather hot-headed, took offense at a remark of a professor and refused to submit to further examination. This altercation festered until it reached the dueling stage and resulted in the student's death.

Still a third version of the duel story says that the meeting with pistols followed the annual commencement ball at Chapel Hill and resulted from an argument started by the rivals on the dance floor. This version says that the meeting followed the midnight ending of the ball and that the fatal bullet pierced Peter's starched shirt front. He was still dressed in his evening clothes.

Whether Peter Dromgoole was shot to death by a jealous rival in love, committed suicide, or fled the Chapel Hill scene for some unexplained reason will now never be known. It is a fact, however, that Peter Dromgoole did come from Virginia to study at Chapel Hill more than a century ago. It is also known that he disappeared in some mysterious fashion and to this day has never been heard from.

It is also known that after the mysterious disappearance of the student, an uncle, the Honorable George C. Dromgoole of Virginia, an alumnus of the University and an attorney of wide reputation, came to Chapel Hill to investigate. After three weeks of futile effort, he returned to his home. In the years following the young man's disappearance, the dueling story came to light.

There were two alleged sources of the story. The first is that one of the three fellow students present for the duel and a witness to the death and burial that followed, broke his pledge of secrecy and talked. Another is that an old slave is said to have overheard an argument between the two rival lovers and the challenge that followed.

The late John Buxton Williams, a well-known citizen of Warren County, was Peter's roommate when the two were enrolled at the University. Williams once wrote a letter that was published in the state press in which he declared that he did not know of any person with whom Peter had had a difference and that he was of the opinion that the popular version of the end of Peter Dromgoole was a figment of someone's wild imagination.

Bruce Cotten, an authority on Dromgoole genealogy and a direct descendant of the grandfather of Peter, wrote an article that appeared in the November, 1924, issue of the *Carolina Magazine,* student literary publication at the University, in which he said that Peter was sighted on the streets of

Wilmington in the summer of 1833 and was reported to have enlisted in the army under the name of his roommate, Williams.

Today visitors who go to the summit of Piney Prospect to enjoy the view down across a vast stretch of wooded lowland, also look with keen interest at the English feudal castle that stands there as if it had grown up a part of the landscape itself. Made of native weathered field stone, with towers and terraces and a "great hall," it is one of the most attractive spots in Piedmont North Carolina.

The castle was started in 1925 by an exclusive social group, the Order of the Gimghouls. A colony of Waldensian stone masons was imported to the Chapel Hill community from Valdese. The construction required many painstaking weeks and months because of the minute detail with which the castle reproduction was created. The place is deliciously grim and ghostly.

The Order of the Gimghouls was established at the University in 1899. The glamour of knighthood and chivalry was infused into the Order at its founding. Students and professors alike have been members. Founders of the Order were Wray Martin of Little Rock, Arkansas; Robert Bingham, former ambassador to the Court of St. James's; W. W. Davies of New London, New Hampshire; Shepherd Bryan of Atlanta; and A. H. Patterson, for many years a professor of physics at the University. The Order lists among its alumni many nationally known figures.

Near Hippol Castle, or Gimghoul Castle, is a semicircular rock seat that was erected by the Order in memory of Dr. Kemp Plummer Battle, one of the presidents of the University. A bronze plate on the seat bears the words: "Erected by the Order of Gimghouls in memory of Kemp Plummer Battle, 1831-1919, who knew and loved these woods as no one else."

The seat was made from a rock pile started by Dr. Battle, who was fond of walking the half mile from the University campus to Piney Prospect during his term of office as University President. At the request of President Battle, persons who visited the hill brought a rock and tossed it on the pile. A large heap developed over the years, and because sophomores were sometimes strict in seeing that freshmen obeyed the tradition, the cairn was also known to University students as Freshman Rock Pile. These assorted rocks were converted into the present seat of beautiful stone masonry in 1925.

Dr. Battle of course knew about the Peter Dromgoole disappearance and the legends that grew up in the wake of the incident. In his *History of the University of North Carolina,* he refers to the matter as the "Dromgoole Myth." He expresses the belief that young Dromgoole was ashamed to go home after he had failed at the University, that he drifted to what was then the turbulent Southwest and was later killed there in a barroom brawl or was assassinated.

What actually did happen to Peter Dromgoole remains, of course, a secret of the ages and another chapter in North Carolina's book of the great unsolved.

Meantime, the fascinating story of the mysterious fate of Peter Dromgoole continues to be passed down to each succeeding student generation at the University of North Carolina in Chapel Hill.

Death and a Strange Ring

ANY collection of mystery stories will quite naturally run towards tragedy. Happiness we understand, or we know where it comes from. Tragedy itself is mysterious to us. And so the unexplained mystery of a young Englishman who lived in Wilmington between the years 1760 and 1768 is quickly classified as a tragedy.

Early in the year 1760, the colonial folk of Wilmington were delighted to welcome there a young Englishman of affable personality and prepossessing appearance. His name was Llewellyn Markwick. He brought with him from England letters of introduction indicating high social position and disclosing the fact that he had relatives among the titled families of the old country. When he arrived in Wilmington he was about twenty-four years old.

Within a few weeks the young stranger completely won the regard and esteem of the leading Wilmington families of that day. His personality made many friendships. In the social realm he was regarded as a prince among entertainers.

When he came to Wilmington Markwick wore a ring of peculiar and striking design. It was in the shape of a snake's body with folds intertwined and the head pointing upward. A large and beautiful diamond was clasped between the snake's jaws. Markwick told his friends the ring was a duplicate of his family crest and that it was the only one in existence.

The young Englishman was a great lover of horses and was the owner of a fine Arabian courser. Hardly a day passed that he was not seen riding through the streets.

One afternoon in the fall of 1760 Markwick went to the stable where he quartered his horse and told the stableman he was going for a short ride. He added that he expected to be back in the early evening. About an hour before Markwick was expected to finish his ride, the horse cantered up without its owner. Nothing was thought of this at the time, for the horse was so well trained that Markwick would often dismount in front of his house, turn the animal toward the stable and tap him on the neck. The horse always returned to the stable.

However, the next morning it was discovered that Markwick had not returned to his home after the ride of the previous evening. Still there was no special alarm or anxiety among his friends. They thought probably he had decided to spend the night with some acquaintance in the country. When he did not return in a day or two, everyone became uneasy. Searching parties were formed and the town was combed, block by block, with no success. A thorough investigation by scores of interested people brought no result. Markwick had disappeared completely. In a law-abiding and orderly community such as Wilmington was in those colonial days, the thought that a murder had been committed was slow in occurring to the Englishman's friends. But after a time consideration was given to the possibility of such a violent end.

Months passed into years. There was not a single clue to the mystery of Markwick's disappearance for eight years.

In the summer of 1768 there was a terrific rainstorm. The deluge continued for twenty-four hours. In the center of town on Third Street between Market and Dock, midway between St. James Church and the Lord Cornwallis headquarters residence, the street became flooded. The level of Third Street at Dock is about fifteen feet higher than at Market, the next intersection northward. The unbroken rush of water down the hill reduced the level of the street several feet.

The weather cleared the following day. One of Markwick's friends was walking in front of the St. James Church site. He happened to glance down and his attention was attracted by something that glittered and shone brightly in the morning sun. He kicked idly at the small object but failed to dislodge it. Then he casually reached down and attempted to pick it up. He met with some difficulty and this aroused his curiosity. He then got down upon his knees in the street to see the object more closely. Only a moment was required to dig away the sand.

To his amazement and horror, the friend discovered why he had been unable to pick up the object, a ring adorned with a diamond. It was firmly gripped by the finger of a bony hand.

Others who happened to be passing by helped to uncover the skeleton. The ring was the one item of identification. When fully cleaned, it was found to be the beautiful and rare gem that Markwick had worn.

On detailed examination the skeleton disclosed that Markwick had apparently been murdered. A lead bullet was found embedded in his skull, which also was fractured from front to rear, the result of some vicious blow. It was reasoned that the young man could have been shot while on horseback. When he fell, his assailants had in all probability made doubly sure he was dead by hitting him on the head with a heavy weapon. The murderers must have then carried the body to the place of burial and there hastily interred it while the residents of the town were peacefully sleeping.

Neither the reason for the slaying nor the identity of the murderers was ever revealed. There is a possibility, of course, that the crime may have been the result of mistaken identity.

An interesting tradition still exists at Wilmington, where story-tellers like to recall that until Third Street was improved with a hardsurface pavement, an indentation where Markwick's skeleton was found always remained in spite of frequent efforts to fill it up to street level.

And we add to North Carolina's list of unsolved mysteries the unfortunate end of Llewellyn Markwick.

The Story of the "Vera Cruz"

SEA STORIES have a flavor all their own, but the North Carolina coast country, by sheer geography, offers additional possibilities for story material. Follow on a map or recall in your mind the peculiar formation of our Tar Heel coast. Trace the coast from the Virginia line to the South Carolina line and note what an astounding maze of sand bars, sounds, rivers, inland waterways, swamps, pocosins, and inlets comprise that country for miles and miles—north and south and to some degree westward and inland. Close study of a detailed map reveals just how extraordinary this coast country is from a structural, topographical, and geographical point of view.

Looking from north to south your eye notes Kill Devil Hill, where the first plane flight took place; Roanoke Island, where the first English colony was attempted in America; and Cape Hatteras, "the graveyard of the Atlantic." There are also such interesting communities as Rodanthe, Avon, Buxton, and Ocracoke. Cape Lookout is there, and Harkers Island, dreaded Cape Fear, and tropical Smith Island.

For this unsolved Tar Heel mystery we go to the Outer Banks region. In other years, because of its formation and geography, this was a smugglers' paradise.

Our story goes back to May 8, 1903. A light easterly wind was blowing, and the pilots at Ocracoke blinked their eyes in surprise to see a bark headed into Ocracoke Inlet. From lookout platforms built in the tops of trees and on the roofs of houses, these pilots daily watched the sea for approaching sails. They were accustomed to seeing schooners head into Ocracoke Inlet, but when they saw a bark through their telescopes, they were amazed.

A gentle easterly wind was blowing and the pilots knew that it was not foul weather that caused this strange craft to head shoreward. So interested were they in this unusual visitor from the sea that the rivalry that ordinarily existed among them in connection with the services they offer was forgotten. Old timers who recall the incident say that the only motor boat on the island at the time, which was owned by that famed Ocracoke pilot, Bill Gaskill, was engaged to meet the vessel. Several pilots, including Gary Bragg, went out.

The bark had dropped anchor in the deep water near the

inlet. For the moment she was safe. But the pilots must have been asking themselves and each other what such a craft was doing in Ocracoke Inlet.

And as the pilots' boat pulled up on the bark, their interest and curiosity grew. Never before had they seen such a spectacle. At some distance the bark seemed to be covered with great black birds, scattered through the rigging, on top of the hatchways and cabins, and literally packed along the rails. But as the Ocracoke pilots drew nearer, they realized that what they saw was hundreds of Negroes. And when the small motor boat pulled close in, these Negroes started jabbering in some strange and foreign tongue. As the pilots came alongside, they saw members of the bark's crew using clubs and heard violent oaths as the crew attempted to quiet the horde of black men.

Finally, in spite of the great din that arose, the pilots negotiated with the skipper of the bark to render him service. It was found that the vessel was the *Vera Cruz,* of Portuguese registration, and that the master's name was Fernando. The skipper said that he was bound from Cape Verde Islands to some down-coast port with 325 passengers, all immigrants, and that he had put in at Ocracoke Inlet to get water. The negotiations further revealed that Captain Fernando also had aboard the bark a great cargo of spirits, Holland gin, in tall stone jugs.

The vessel lay at anchor for a day or two while the rather deliberate business of taking on water went forward. Finally the day for sailing arrived, and the pilots went aboard to direct the vessel back to the seaways. But just before weighing anchor, the wind shifted to the northeast and soon a spanking good breeze was blowing. At the wheel was Captain Bill Gaskill, who had been chosen as helmsman. Other Ocracokers were also aboard the vessel at the time.

Now these pilots knew well the art of handling afore and aft sailboats under any sort of circumstance, but they were a bit bewildered aboard the bark, not so much by the square sails, which had been unreefed, but by the confusion and the shouts of the master—in poor English and a combination of Portuguese and Spanish.

With the sails set, Captain Fernando suddenly shouted and motioned the pilot at the wheel to starboard. The breeze at just that moment increased, and instead of clearing a dangerous shoal that exists there in the inlet, the *Vera Cruz* floundered right on it.

Portsmouth Life-Saving Station on the south side of the inlet came to the rescue. It was at that time the nearest station, for the Ocracoke station was not constructed until a year after this incident.

Captain Fernando and his supercargo—supercargo being the title given to an official aboard ship who takes care of cargo, or represents the owner—came to Ocracoke. They said they wanted to send a telegram to representatives in some northern port. Meantime, the situation was also reported by wire to officials of the cutter service, and the *Boutwell* of New Bern set out for Ocracoke Inlet with revenue agents aboard. Captain Fernando and his supercargo had left the chief officer aboard the *Vera Cruz* to attend to cargo and to help get the 325 passengers ashore. And Ocracokers who were on hand said that he used a goodly portion of the Holland gin from the cargo in conjunction with these duties.

This gin, in tall stone jugs, was given as a present to many natives of the Banks and was sold cheaply to others. People who went on board the floundered ship to barter for coins, trinkets, and souvenirs came away in many instances with the tall stone jugs. And some of these, emptied—odd of shape and size—are still to be found on Ocracoke Island.

One of the passengers who was ill died while the vessel was in the inlet and was buried on Dry Shoal Island.

Captain Fernando and his supercargo, who went to Ocracoke to send telegrams to the owners, changed their minds when they arrived there. On the island they engaged Dan Tolson and Lum Gaskill to take them to Belhaven, which was the nearest railroad terminus. They made the trip aboard the *Relief,* a well-known sailboat in the Ocracoke area in that day. The pair from the *Vera Cruz* paid $50 for the trip, an enormous sum for such a charter at that time.

Meantime all the passengers were removed from the *Vera Cruz.* Residents of Ocracoke and Portsmouth continued to barter with the mate of the ship, and there was considerable drinking of the Holland gin from the tall stone jugs, according to the story.

It was a day or so later that the *Boutwell* arrived from New Bern, with the government officials aboard. These officials found that only fifty of the 325 Negro passengers had passports. In the group were sixteen women and some of them had given birth to babies since they left their island homes. This number of Negroes had never before been quartered on Ocracoke Island or at any other place along the Banks. But the weather was warm and many of the passengers slept out in the open. Others occupied cow stalls, sheds, and outbuildings of all kinds.

None of the passengers had money or items of value. They had turned all their valuables over to Captain Fernando when the *Vera Cruz* sailed—for safe-keeping. The skipper had all these valuables in a black bag, and the black bag went with him when he set out for Belhaven in the chartered sailboat.

And then the news came back to the island that Captain Fernando had boarded a northbound Norfolk and Southern train at Belhaven instead of sending telegrams and transacting the business there that he had indicated was necessary. With him into a temporary oblivion went the black bag with the valuables of his luckless 325 Negro passengers.

Some years later a seaman aboard an ice boat which sailed from North Carolina was on the Kennebec River in Maine and there met another seaman from the whaling town of New Bedford. This seaman supplied some further details on what happened to Captain Fernando. The New Bedford seaman said that the Portuguese captain smuggled himself out of New Bedford aboard a whaling vessel, hidden in one of the empty oil casks. At any rate that was the word that came back to Ocracoke.

The story developed as passengers and crew were questioned. Captain Fernando had promised his passengers before they sailed that he would see that they entered America— passports or no passports. Well, he kept his word as to that. But those who had no legal documents for entering this country were subsequently deported back to their island homes.

And then, when some pieces of the story were put together like sections of a jig-saw puzzle, it became apparent that the villainous Captain Fernando had every intention of deliberately wrecking his bark on the shoal in Ocracoke Inlet. It was a desperate move after another plan had failed.

Islanders recalled that for many days before the arrival of

the *Vera Cruz* there was an unusually large number of down-east fishing smacks in the ocean adjacent to Ocracoke Island. The sails of a score or more could be counted for several days. Now it can be taken for granted that these fishermen were waiting for the Portuguese bark. The bark failed to keep its rendezvous at some fixed time, it was thought, and when it finally did arrive—late—the ocean was empty of smacks. It was then that Captain Fernando took the reckless way out of the difficulty that had overtaken him.

Some of the Negro passengers on the *Vera Cruz,* whose passport papers were in order so that they could remain in this country, settled in the swamp lands of Eastern North Carolina.

So the *Vera Cruz* was apparently engaged in traffic with human contraband. The story is reminiscent of the old slave-trade days when "black ivory," as Negro slave cargoes were called, was brought into this country through North Carolina waters. There was also a period of smuggling Chinese into this country, mostly on the west coast but in some instances on our own coast. There were stringent laws governing this business, but along our Outer Banks the traffic in human beings continued until the war of the sixties.

North Carolina had laws with which to handle slave-smugglers. An ancient copy of "Shipmaster's Assistant and Commercial Digest" prescribes severe penalties under our state laws. Masters of vessels, or any persons belonging to a vessel, were liable in cases where slaves were smuggled in or out of North Carolina ports. Of course, there were national laws, also, which prevailed and were applied to these practices.

Before the war, this human contraband was taken usually

to the West Indies and brought in along the North Carolina coast and further southward by "runners." A slave's life was not highly valued by the slave runners who were attempting to bring them into this country. With the approach of a revenue cutter, the "black ivory" was frequently weighted alive and dumped overboard to drown.

And so, as late as 1903, a newer version of what was once an illicit slave trade bobbed up again at Ocracoke on the Outer Banks. The mysterious behavior of Captain Fernando and his crew, his apparently deliberate effort to wreck his bark on the Ocracoke Inlet shoals, and his subsequent flight from the scene, make another chapter in the collection of intriguing sea tales from the Carolina coast.

The Devil's Tramping Ground

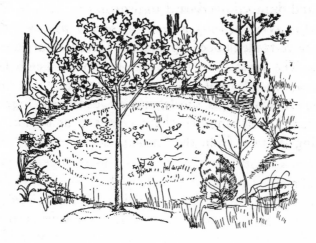

CHATHAM COUNTY, smilingly known for a tradi-
tional rabbit population, also has a lively unsolved
mystery—a mystery of nature.

Chatham, an historic county, was settled in 1771 by
planters who moved in from the Cape Fear region. Both the
county and the county seat, Pittsboro, were named for the
Earl of Chatham, William Pitt, champion of colonial rights
in the British Parliament.

The present Chatham County courthouse was built at
Pittsboro in 1882 at a time when that village was known as
Chatham Court House. Cornwallis spent a night at Chatham

Court House in the course of his march to Wilmington after the Battle of Guilford Court House. David Fanning and his band of Tories once raided the town while a court-martial was in progress and captured forty-four persons as a part of Fanning's program of terrorizing that area during the Revolutionary War period. So Chatham County, rich in history, looks back over nearly two centuries of vibrant life.

Against this background we have an unsolved mystery, a curiosity of nature that has grown into a legend, has attracted thousands of visitors to the scene of the phenomenon, and has brought forth hundreds of explanations as to its origin.

We go ten miles from Siler City to a point in western Chatham County for the scene of this strange story. Here we find a cleared path, in a perfect circle, in a grove of trees on the L. R. Down property. This path has existed as far back as the memory of man—and it has always been just as it is found today, without so much as a sprig of vegetation growing in the pathway. The spot is just off a rural highway and has no more official marking or designation than a state highway sign at Harper Cross Roads, one mile distant, pointing to the odd spot.

It's the Devil's Tramping Ground, the Chatham natives say. And the story is that the Devil goes there to walk in circles as he thinks up new means of causing trouble for humanity. There, sometime during the dark of night, the Majesty of the Underworld of Evil silently tramps around and around that bare circle—thinking, plotting, and planning against good, and in behalf of wrong.

So far as is known, no person has ever spent the night there to disprove that this is what happens and that this is what keeps grass, weeds, and other vegetation worn clean and bare from the circle called the Devil's Tramping Ground.

The cleared spot, surrounded by trees, comprises a perfect circle with a forty-foot diameter. The path itself is about a foot wide and is barren of any obstruction—growing or otherwise. A certain variety of wire grass grows inside the circle in a limited fashion and residents of that neighborhood say that any attempts to transplant any of it have met with failure. Broomsedge, moss, and grasses grow on the outer edge of the circular path, but not inside the circle.

Persons who visit the spot frequently place sticks and stones in the path and sometimes tie sticks there, anchoring them with strings across the cleared band of earth, but the path is always found clear the next day. This, the story has it, indicates that the Devil kicks the obstacles aside on his nightly perambulations.

Many have been the explanations offered for this oddity of nature—this perfect circle that year after year ever remains clear of any growth whatsoever.

One of the oldest and best-known of the legendary explanations for the Devil's Tramping Ground is that hundreds of years ago when many Indian tribes roamed the section that is now Chatham County—known then to the Indians as the Great Flats—the tribes would meet at periodic occasions in celebrations and feasts. The spot that is today known as the Devil's Tramping Ground was a principal meeting place for these occasions of festivity, assembly, and counciling.

Thousands of these first Americans would gather and the braves would hold their vigorous war dances. The treading of their feet wore a circle in the earth as the Indians called on The Great Spirit in the Happy Hunting Ground to give them success in their enterprises of war. And their God has kept, as a token and a monument to these faithful Indian braves, the circle that their moccasined feet wore bare as they danced about their camp fire in supplication to him and in defiance of their enemies.

And there is another Indian legend about the spot, and this one ties in with the Lost Colony of Roanoke Island—as do many Tar Heel Indian legends.

Years before the first white settlers came to this region, two rival Indian tribes met in battle at the present scene of the Devil's Tramping Ground and after a short but bitter conflict stained the ground thereabouts with the blood of the dead and wounded. The leader of one of the tribes was named Chief Croatan and he was killed in the engagement. With the leader of this tribe gone and casualties severe, the remaining warriors gathered the women and children of the tribe together, and with brief but impressive ceremony buried their chief in a spot that is today the exact center of the Devil's Tramping Ground. They named the spot Croatan in honor of their fallen chief and then fled eastward to the North Carolina coast to avoid further contact with their superior enemy and to start the life of their weakened tribe anew in another place.

This particular legend contends further that it was this spot—named Croatan after the dead Chief Croatan—that the members of the Lost Colony were headed for when they carved the word "Croatoan" on a tree and left the site of Sir Walter Raleigh's colony on Roanoke Island, to be forever swallowed up in oblivion.

And, according to this second Indian story, since Chief Croatan was buried there, The Great Spirit has kept bare the circle around the grave, down through the years, in mourning for the loss of a faithful chief and a great leader.

There are still other explanations to be had in the western Chatham countryside. Natives there will tell you that the bare and circular path was made of the hoofs of many horses and mules as they circled to supply the power for grinding cane at a one-time molasses mill—and that the tread was so pronounced that vegetation has never returned. Other paths made at other treadmills pulled by horses have not, however, borne out this theory.

Legend further has it that no birds build their nests in trees adjacent to this spot and that wild game is never found there. Lawyer L. P. Dixon of Siler City tells of a certain possum-hunting incident. When the hunting party approached the Devil's Tramping Ground, he says, the dogs lowered their tails, gave up the warm trail they were following, and dropped in behind their masters to have the safety and protection of human beings.

Years ago travellers never dared to pass the spot after nightfall.

Perhaps the best explanation, and certainly the most scientific approach to a solution of the mystery came first from Harry Davis, curator of the North Carolina State Museum. Curator Davis was in that area on one occasion, with Dr. J. L. Stuckey, state geologist, when they were testing wells for their sodium chloride content—and sodium chloride is common salt.

While in the vicinity they encountered the remains of ancient salt licks that had been used by buffalo and deer— and buffalo and deer did roam the Chatham terrain in days long gone. In the area, Mr. Davis noted several instances of vegetation that thrives on moisture from brackish water such as is found along the coast. There is other definite evidence of a pretty heavy salt content in some parts of that section.

Mr. Davis thinks that the Devil's Tramping Ground is nothing more or less than a spot of earth that is sufficiently loaded with salt to prevent ordinary vegetation from thriving there.

And this horse-back opinion of the curator of the Raleigh Museum has been backed up by recent scientific investigations. But even these investigations did not solve the mystery.

W. A. Bridges, of the W. A. Bridges Laboratory at Wilson, and Dr. I. E. Miles, director of the Soil Testing Division of the North Carolina Department of Agriculture, ran tests on samples of soil taken from the middle of the circular path. I made arrangements for the samples of soil to be taken by W. B. Morgan, Siler City newspaper man, after a Devil's Tramping Ground radio program that I presented had produced such a widespread interest over the state.

The tests by both chemists showed that the soil in the path of the Devil's Tramping Ground is sterile. Mr. Bridges' report said in part: "Although there may be other factors of a physical nature that would make this a sterile soil, our findings show that plant life will not be supported on a soil that is so acid and so low in the necessary soil nutriments."

But the mystery that remains in the face of that scientific finding presents the questions: With the soil in this curious spot too poor to support plant life, why the circular path with grass and trees growing right up to its edge? Soil rebuilds itself over a period of time; so why has this spot remained unfruitful as far back as we have recorded history, as far back as the Indian age and even to the time two hundred years ago when settlers first came into this territory? So science deepens our mystery as it seeks to solve it.

Meantime, the natives of western Chatham and many of the thousands of people who go there to examine the curious spot adhere strongly to the belief that the Devil himself has reserved that spot of land for his personal use.

I heard a story from Dr. Will Long of Graham which bears out Harry Davis' contention that the explanation of the Devil's Tramping Ground lies in a salt content of the earth there. Dr. Long told me of a strange sight seen in Chatham County in his youth. Passing a certain area there one day, he saw sheep come pouring up out of the ground in a long chain of scurrying animals—an amazing sight indeed!

Investigation revealed that the sheep were down in an old salt lick of the sort that Mr. Davis said was used in other ages by buffalo and deer, back when the Indians knew the area as the Great Flats. Animals—wild and domestic—that had roamed those hillsides for years had licked at the salt deposit and eaten it away until a great cave had been carved out in the earth. The sheep of Dr. Long's story, like many an animal before them, had gone into the opening for a few licks at the salty formation there.

There are two man-made scars at the Devil's Tramping Ground. They are holes in the center of the Tramping Ground and they were made there by unknown vandals and treasure seekers who dug there as a result of still another legend that has grown up about the place—indicating that there is a buried treasure under the eerie spot. There is no available explanation as to the source of this theory about hidden wealth.

Just who first discovered the spot is not known. There is evidence that the story of the Devil and his nightly meditative walks have been handed along for more than 150 years, from one generation of residents in that section to another.

There is no evidence that the Devil—if he still goes tramp-tramping there in a circle in the dark of night—has ever resented the curiosity that has brought thousands to his tramping ground for a possible invasion of his privacy. But if he takes his nightly walks in Chatham, and if he thinks as he tramps, and if this thinking is as evil as one would suppose, then many of the world's woes have been generated in lovely, rural Chatham County.

The Plant that was Lost for a Hundred Years

THIS series of North Carolina mysteries has so far presented stories of people, of places, of ships, and of treasure. Now we add even more variety and present a North Carolina mystery in which the central figure is a dainty flowering plant. The story is about a man, too, and his interest in this particular plant, but the mystery itself is essentially a floral presentation.

And what better setting could we find for such a story than the land of Tarheelia, where we have a floral and botanical parade unmatched in any other state and ranging from the beautiful rhododendron covering the mountain slopes to the rare Venus fly-trap near the coast.

There is in North Carolina, for instance, a certain flame azalea that is found nowhere else on earth save in this state and in a section of India. And so we have here a state unique among the eastern states—in botany as in other realms. North Carolina possesses within her borders the best examples of the most diverse vegetations. As B. W. Wells, professor of botany at N. C. State College, once put it: "Whoever the men were who designed the geographical biscuit cutter which sliced out the Old North State, they succeeded so well botanically that one might think of them as possessed with less political sense than vegetational acumen." At any rate, in one east-west state unit those designers managed to include the finest examples of the mountain plants of the southern Appalachians, constituting an extension of the Canadian balsam fir forest, along with the southern low country plants which range north in swamps and pocosins from the Gulf of Mexico.

So, in a very real sense, North Carolina unites Canada and Florida in the world of plants, although the state lies east and west. When snow hangs heavy on the spruce of the mountains, warm breezes fresh from the Gulf Stream fan the palmetto trees of Smith Island.

Mystery and detective work do not belong alone to the realms of murder and sabotage. There is also a record of some botanical sleuthing in this book of North Carolina mysteries. The object of the search of our botanical Sherlock Holmes was a shy little plant, an evergreen ground-cover with a leaf like that of galax and a dainty, cream-white flower that blooms in early spring. It was lost for a hundred years and was the object of a continuous forty-year search before it was rediscovered in North Carolina.

Our story starts—strangely enough—with a French botanist named André Michaux, who was born in 1746 and died in 1802. Michaux was an untiring collector of American flora. He visited this country in 1788 and spent considerable time in Western North Carolina, collecting specimens in the mountain country there.

Apparently André Michaux had all the typical enthusiasms of the French. In 1794, he climbed to the top of Grandfather Mountain and exultantly sang the "Marseillaise," believing he stood on the highest point in America.

Delighted with the botanical specimens that he found in the Appalachian range in North Carolina, he spent some of the time during his prolonged stay teaching the North Carolina mountaineers how to prepare ginseng root for the profitable China trade.

When he returned to Paris, Michaux took with him, in his elaborate collection, one faded, incomplete specimen which bore a label indicating that it came from the high mountains of Carolina and was a new genus. In the journal that he kept of his trip and collection, the French scientist gave elaborate, but somewhat misleading, directions so that future botanists might also locate the plant in the "high mountains of Carolina."

Some decades later a young American botanist named Asa Gray was at the University of Michigan. In 1858 Asa Gray sailed for Europe to examine there the American flora as it existed at that time in the principal herbaria of Europe. Arriving in Paris, the American botanist studied the collection of André Michaux.

There he encountered the little specimen labeled as from the "high mountains of Carolina." The dainty specimen bewitched Asa Gray, and beginning then and there, he took up the trail of this plant, which carried him through forty years of sleuthing and searching. The American botanist worked out one elusive clue after another until his faith was finally vindicated late in his career as a botanist. He hailed the triumphant discovery as the most satisfactory episode in his long and fruitful life.

Enthusiastic over the specimen that he found in Paris in the Michaux collection, Gray took the liberty of naming the plant in honor of Charles Wilkins Short, whom he had never met but for whom he had unbounded admiration. He called the plant *Shortia galacifolia*. Short lived between 1795 and 1863; a friendship had grown up between the two men, based on a voluminous correspondence about their mutual interest—botany. Short never saw a specimen of the flower named for him.

And so the shy little mountain plant caught the fancy and stirred the imagination of Asa Gray. It was a case of botanical love at first sight.

To go back to the story of the search, Gray returned to America with two friends, and started his first quest for *Shortia galacifolia* in 1841. They proceeded to the "high mountains of Carolina" as recommended. Their hunt took them along the sides and over the crests of Roan, Iron, Grandfather, Black, and other mountains. But it was a fruitless trip. And after it was over, Gray wrote to Sir William J. Hooker, "We were unsuccessful in our search for a remarkable undescribed plant with a habit of Pyrola and the foliage of Galax."

Michaux's directions had been fairly specific, but his continual references to the "high mountains" misled the botany detective. The Frenchman had written:

"The head of the Keowee is the junction of two torrents of considerable size which flow in cascades from the high mountains. On descending from the junction of these two torrents with the river to one's left in the mountains which face north on the right, one finds at about 200-300 feet from the junction, a path formed by the Indian hunters. It leads to a brook where one recognizes the site of an Indian village by the peach trees which still exist in the midst of the underbrush. Continuing on this path one soon reaches the mountains and one finds this plant which covers the ground along with *Epigaea repens*."

Again carefully studying these and other notes, Gray in 1843 resumed the search, but once more he kept to the peaks and never came within many miles of the plant's restricted habitat.

The mystery infected other botanists. Dr. John Torrey first suggested in 1852 that *Shortia* might be an early spring plant and that it might disappear after flowering. John Carey urged Dr. Gray to ascertain the name and whereabouts of Michaux's old guide, John Davenport, in an effort to track down the elusive plant.

Rediscovery came through seventeen-year-old George McQueen Hyams of Statesville, who found *Shortia* growing on the banks of the Catawba River near Marion, in McDowell County, at an altitude much lower than Gray had anticipated. Hyams' father was a herbalist but did not know the plant; and it was eighteen months before he sent a specimen to a friend, Joseph W. Congdon, of West Greenwich, R. I.

Congdon then wrote Dr. Gray, telling him he thought he had *Shortia,* and sent the specimen to him.

The forty-year search was over, and Gray was triumphant and jubilant. In his life many honors had come to him, but he considered them as naught compared to discovery of the little mountain plant he held in his hands at last. He wrote, "If you will come here, I can show you what will delight your eyes and cure you effectively of the skeptical spirit you used to have about *Shortia galacifolia.* . . . Think of that: My long faith rewarded at last."

The botanical Sherlock Holmes now organized a new party and came to North Carolina, where he saw with his own eyes the rare flower. It was, however, not in bloom.

Gray never saw it bloom in its native habitat.

Still he persisted in trying to locate the place described by Michaux, and in a letter to Dr. Short's daughter, he optimistically noted: "But I am not yet sixty-nine years old, and I hope to try once more."

It remained for Dr. Charles Sprague Sargent to rediscover the place where Michaux had grubbed out the original plants. In 1886 after a hard day's work he examined a specimen, sent it to Gray, who identified it as the elusive *Shortia.*

But the mystery deepened. Sargent and his party had traveled over rough mountain country, and he could not recall where he had found the plant. Nevertheless, the trail was hot, and Frank E. Boynton, of Highlands, and his brother were sent back over the route.

Boynton remembered that Sargent had crossed Bear Camp Creek, a little stream flowing into the Horse Pasture River, which enters the Keowee. Here they dug up *Shortia;* and at long last a specimen was sent to Gray from the very spot described by Michaux on December 8, 1788. The old path noted by Michaux in his clues was still discernible.

The restricted habitat of *Shortia* is not explained. Dr. Wells says *Shortia* is a lingering survival of another botanical age on the way to extinction. But in the Toxaway country of North Carolina, it grows profusely, mostly in places difficult of access. One collector wrote: "No idea of the beauty of this plant can be formed until it has been seen in its native home. The mass of glossy green and white, once seen, can never be forgotten." This was the sight Gray was never to see.

Shortia as a rule grows under the shade of rhododendrons and tall *Kalmias*. Blooming period is at its height about March 20. It has been successfully transplanted and in nurseries is known as Oconee Bells and Little Colt's Foot. Webster's *Unabridged Dictionary* describes *Shortia* as a perennial herb, with smooth basal leaves and a solitary white flower. There are just two kinds, the variety growing in the mountains of Western North Carolina and a variety that grows in Japan. "The American species," Webster's *Dictionary* adds, "is one of the rarest of plants."

The complete truth of the dictionary statement can, perhaps, be gathered from this story of the plant's disappearance, or hiding, and its eventual rediscovery. Rare it was and rare it still is.

Before he died, Gray asked that, of all the 25,000 botanical specimens he classified, *Shortia galacifolia* cover his grave at Cambridge, Massachusetts.

The Strange Hoof-Marks at Bath

~~~~~~

NO collection of unsolved North Carolina mysteries would be complete without the curious Tar Heel legend of the Strange Hoof-Marks at Bath, sometimes called the Magic Horse Tracks.

The locale of this story is near the historic town of Bath, a little Beaufort County riverside village of some four hundred persons. It is the oldest town in North Carolina and was at one time capital of the Colonial Province. The town was the seat of old Bath County, named for the Earl of Bath, one of the Lords Proprietors.

The oldest standing church in North Carolina, and one of

the oldest in America—St. Thomas Episcopal Church—is at Bath. It was built in 1734. The vestry for this church was organized in 1701 and was partly maintained from England.

Bath has changed but little in the last century. Its beauty lies in its old homes, which depict an early architecture of charm and mellow antiquity. The people there live by fishing and farming.

Charles Eden, the governor of the Province from 1714 until his death in 1722, for a time maintained his capital at Bath. The town is said to have once served as the headquarters of Blackbeard, the pirate.

The little village is on a peninsula formed by Bath and Back creeks. From the south end of the town's main street is a view of the mouth of Bath Creek, opening into the broad, blue Pamlico River. Along the banks of the creek are piles of stone, ballast rock from ships of early colonists.

Approximately a mile from Bath, as you approach it from the west, natives will direct you to a side road that leads off into the woods about 250 yards. On the left of this side road is the beginning of a wood road or trail. About ten yards down this trail is a series of round, shallow depressions in the ground, about as big as a large saucer or small plate.

What you see appears to be just a series of holes in the earth. But there is more to the story. Examination quickly reveals no leaves, pine needles, or trash of any kind in the depressions. And although grass grows all around the spot, none grows in or about these holes.

And local history reveals that these holes have been there, empty and bare, for nearly a century and a half. If they are filled with earth or woods debris, they are found to be empty and clean some hours later or by the next morning.

The skeptical have often tried this, and the holes have always reappeared or restored themselves just as before.

Ed Cutler, a near-by farmer, once said that the pits were made into a mudwallow for his hogs, but that even then the depressions in the earth refused to vanish.

In the community today are many adults who tried filling the pits with earth when they were children on their way to school, only to find empty holes again when they came back by the spot in the afternoon, on their way home.

And so for nearly a hundred and fifty years, these holes have persisted, always as fresh as ever, and firmly resisting any effort to mar or eliminate them.

Where did this strange sequence of pits in the face of the earth come from?

They are the hoof-marks of a horse, according to a curious Tar Heel legend. And they cannot be effaced.

According to the legend a rather profane gentleman of Bath named Jesse Elliott, with several madcap companions, was given to horse racing on Sundays. One Sunday in August of 1802, as he galloped down the race lane, Elliott shouted to his horse, "Take me in a winner or take me to hell."

With that exclamation, a penitent companion later reported, the horse dug its hoofs into the soft earth in two mighty leaps and hurled the rider against a near-by tree, killing him instantly.

The marks the horse made in that instance still remain to intrigue men and women who have been seeing them and wondering about them for a century and a half.

The Beaufort County community took the death of the gay young blood of the neighborhood as a solemn warning from on high, and Sabbath-breaking in that section forthwith ceased, according to the legend. The minister at Bath, who had been delivering vehement protests from his pulpit at the manner in which the band of roistering blades cursed, gambled, and raced their horses on Sunday, took quick advantage of the death of the young man and exhorted God-fearing congregations about the wild and scandalous goings-on among the young people and the inevitable dire results—which in this one instance, he contended, had been demonstrated.

The minister—and he was rector of the old St. Thomas church in Bath—probably gave a title to the incident, which has since persisted. The five shallow pits in the earth, he said, were footprints made by "a man on his way to hell."

And so, according to the legend, the hoof-marks of the spirited horse have remained as a reminder of the tragic fate which overtakes wild young sinners like Jesse Elliott.

Today the series of five marks in the earth is lined up in an irregular path beside an old stump. This is the stump of the tree that is supposed to have figured in young Elliott's fatal accident. It was apparently a large tree, although the stump is now much decayed and does not show very high above the ground.

Embellishments of the story appear from time to time in the Bath area. There is, for instance, a local theory that a stick thrust into one of the depressions and left there will eventually disappear completely.

There is a version of the story that comes down by word of mouth that the man against whom Elliott was racing, and who was leading Elliott in the contest, looked back in a flash of a glance over his shoulder just in time to see both horse and rider killed, and that the contestant rode off to get help but upon return found both the dead man and the dead horse gone, and neither was ever seen or heard from again.

Some years ago a motion picture newsreel company heard about the mysterious footprints and sent a cameraman there to get some shots. Earl Harrell, the cameraman, arrived at Bath and talked to many of the natives. One man told him that he had seen some chickens feeding around the spot one day and that they would eat all about the depressions but would touch nothing in the pits themselves, even when food was put there expressly to tempt them.

So Harrell thought that might be a good angle for his film shots. He borrowed some chickens from a farmer near by and bought a quantity of mixed-grain chicken feed. Scattering the feed all about the hoof-marks—inside and out— he set the chickens free and started his cameras rolling.

The chickens ate every grain of feed on the outside of the depressions, but they wouldn't touch a single grain in the depressions proper. The film showed the chickens standing beside the shallow holes, heads cocked to look inside at the feed waiting there, but never did one of them venture to peck so much as a grain of feed out of one of the five holes— even after the ground round about had been picked clean.

The cameraman was so impressed that he decided to try out the theory that trash and earth put in the holes would disappear. So he made arrangements to spend an additional day in the vicinity. He scraped up quite a pile of leaves, twigs, small stones and dirt, and covered the area over with a layer of this debris. Then he carefully placed a network of black thread over the whole spot. When he returned the next morning the holes themselves were open, clean and clear. The net was still in place, and the material remained intact all about—except where it had been just over and on top of the holes.

Conservative natives, who offer no explanation for the depressions, or the strange behavior that attends them, say that sometimes it takes a week for trash placed in the pits to disappear but that when it does disappear it goes suddenly and completely. Nothing ever covers the tracks for very long. In all the history of these marks there has been no shelter above the spot to protect it from the washings of rain and weather. The earth all about is bare—as already reported herein—and is very firm.

Through two men alone the presence of the tracks has been traced back for more than a hundred years. J. S. Mann of Middleton once reported a conversation on a Southern Railway train. He was returning home from the University of North Carolina in 1881. He was a freshman at the University at that time. On the train he met a Dr. Chopin of Aurora, Beaufort County, and Dr. Chopin told him about the strange hoof-marks. Mann was skeptical, but Dr. Chopin said he had been seeing and knowing about the marks for fifty years at that time.

A few years later, Mr. Mann reported in a letter on the subject that he had had an occasion to visit Bath and had looked up the strange phenomenon. Still later, he took his wife and children to see the hoof-marks; and at the time of his letter, Mr. Mann vouched for the presence of the depressions for fifty-four years of his life. So between Dr. Chopin and Mr. Mann, more than a hundred years of the presence of the strange ineradicable marks in the earth are vouched for.

Bill Sharpe, who heads the News Bureau of the North

Carolina Department of Conservation and Development and who still looks at things with that cultivated and hard-bitten skepticism of a newspaperman, thinks that maybe the earth there contains some form of soluble rock—salt, lime, or otherwise—and that through their dissolving under the surface of the earth there has been a constant drainage into these depressions, with perhaps some suction that would take soil or debris into the earth. If, on the other hand, there is any great amount of drainage or suction, it would seem that over the years the holes would get deeper or bigger.

Residents of Beaufort County snort at any idea other than that a horse, taking a man to the devil on his own instructions, made those indelible marks in the earth's surface.

After I had presented a radio broadcast on "The Strange Hoof-Marks at Bath" in September, 1946, I had a letter from a classmate at the University of North Carolina, Galen Elliott, park and playground director at Lancaster, South Carolina. Galen had heard the broadcast, and he gave me the information that Jesse Elliott was his great-great-grand-father. He also supplied some facts on the hoof-prints story, from the Elliott family point of view.

The Lancaster descendant and a former fellow student said that Jesse and Seth Elliott, brothers, came to America from England and settled west of Bath in Beaufort County. Seth moved on to a new location and was never heard from again. Jesse married and had a son named William.

With respect to the tragedy that caused the hoof-prints, Galen Elliott said in his letter:

"Here is the story as told to my father by the slave darky, Uncle Washington, who groomed the horse as a young slave and who was still living at the time my father was growing up. Uncle Washington said that the horse was a beautiful and spirited bay mare and could run like a deer. He said he had ridden her many times before the accident and afterwards, so the horse was not killed at the time of the accident, as many of the stories have it. Neither was Jesse Elliott racing on Sunday. According to Uncle Washington, he was giving the mare a workout—running her along a woods road late in the afternoon of Christmas Eve day in 1813, getting her ready for the big annual race which was to be held two weeks later on old Christmas Day, January 6. The track was some eight miles from the site of the accident in the vicinity of what is now Hunter's Bridge. The horse was running at full speed when something frightened her, causing her to pitch and stop suddenly. This caused the rider to be thrown headfirst over the horse's head, his own head striking a large pine with such force that it split his skull.

"So the date that had been handed down to us, i.e., Christmas Eve day, 1813, was not Sunday, but Friday.

"As to why the hoof-prints remain, I haven't the slightest idea. I do know they are there, and have been since the time of the tragedy. The tree itself was still standing when my father was a young man, with the side of the tree that Jesse Elliott's head struck dead and the rest still living. Today the tree is gone, with just slight signs of the old stump remaining.

"As far as I know there is no natural explanation as to why the horse tracks have remained in the light sandy loam soil there for all these decades. I do know that wells dug in the same soil in the same community less than fifty years ago, and later abandoned, have left no trace. Today they are completely filled up, so that you can't even find the spot where the well once existed and produced water."

That is the family version, passed down through the line of descendants by word of mouth.

Factual reporting does indicate that the depressions have been there apparently unchanged for nearly a hundred and fifty years. And it's true enough that the marks are in a position of sequence to indicate a pattern that might have been made by a running horse. They suggest, with the assistance of some imagination, that a horse, running at top speed, bumped into a tree at the spot, and was thrown to the right.

The basic facts of the legend—from the reported death of Jesse Elliott to the present day—are largely vouched for by many reputable people. The folk legend is continuous. And that's the strange story of the Hoof-Marks at Bath.

The Lost Colony

NO series of unsolved North Carolina mysteries could possibly be complete without including the story of the Lost Colony and Virginia Dare. That was the very first of all American mysteries, and it took place here in Tarheelia, on Roanoke Island, down in the North Carolina sound country. And while it is the oldest of American and North Carolina mysteries, it has remained stubbornly unsolved after nearly four centuries.

Interest in the Lost Colony has been accentuated in recent years through the presentation each summer—on that very spot on Roanoke Island where the Lost Colony made its headquarters and where Virginia Dare was born—of Paul Green's immortal dramatization of the story.

The intensely interesting Lost Colony chapter from our early history belongs to the drama-packed Tar Heel coast country and is a part of the exploration and attempted first settlement of Roanoke Island from 1584 to 1587.

With the blessing and assistance of Queen Elizabeth of England, Sir Walter Raleigh sent two ships west from England on April 27, 1584, well furnished with men and with food, to explore the North American coast with the idea of founding an English empire beyond the seas to be colonized by the English people. The company of explorers landed on the North Carolina coast on July 13, 1584.

The explorers climbed to the top of hills (so described that they could be the Nags Head dunes of today), discovered that they were on a barrier island, and moved on to the northern end of Roanoke Island where they were entertained in a palisaded Indian village by friendly natives. The group eventually returned to England, taking with them two Indians to help convey the story of this new land.

Queen Elizabeth was pleased; the undefined territory was given the name Virginia to memorialize the Virgin Queen; and Sir Walter Raleigh was the chief lord of the new area.

The next spring Raleigh sent out another colony of 108 persons to Roanoke Island. This expedition sailed from Plymouth on April 9, 1585, in seven ships. In the party were men of varied talents, including artists, scientists, and persons of humbler talents. The two Indians also returned to their native haunts. After a stop at Puerto Rico, where the expedition picked up needed supplies and breeding animals for their new colony, the explorers reached what is now

Ocracoke on June 26. They explored the coastal islands and adjacent mainland and finally, on July 27, anchored off Roanoke Island. Meantime they sought to strike terror into the hearts of the Indians by burning an Indian village in retaliation for the theft of a silver cup stolen by one of the Indians.

A colony was established on the north end of the island and Ralph Lane was made governor. Letters that went back home to England when boats returned for supplies indicated how greatly impressed were the colonists with the vast and unknown extent of the American continent as it stretched away to the west.

Lane built a fort near the shore on the east side of the island, between the north point of the island and a creek that had a mouth large enough to provide anchorage for the boats. This is the present Fort Raleigh National Historical site and the Waterside Theatre, where "The Lost Colony" production is to be seen each year. The remains of this fort were visible as late as 1896 and can be described by many of the older natives on Roanoke Island. The skilled laborers of the expedition made brick, sawed boards, and built carefully. Pieces of this early brick could be found on the fort site as late as 1860.

The colonists' relations with the Indians became more and more strained, until by June of 1586 a state of actual warfare existed, cutting off the source of most of the native supplies. The ships that had gone to England were delayed in returning. The colonists were in a desperate predicament by the time Sir Francis Drake anchored off the coast with a fleet of twenty-three ships on June 9, 1586. Drake offered assistance to the colonists. He said that he would leave a ship, new skilled help, and supplies, or that he would take the entire expedition back to England with his fleet.

Lane was loath to give up the Roanoke Island project and decided to stay, with new supplies. And then, while the supplies were being made ready, a storm struck, causing Drake's fleet considerable damage. So, in the face of troubled conditions in Europe and America, and the unaccountable delay in the arrival of the supply ships from home, Lane finally asked for passage to England and Drake sailed on June 18, taking the colonists home with him.

Shortly after Drake sailed with the colonists, the supply ships from England *did* arrive at Roanoke Island and searched in vain for the colonists. Finding no one and nothing—save the desolate settlement—and not wishing to lose possession of the land for England, Sir Richard Grenville, in charge of the supply fleet, left fifteen men on Roanoke Island, with provisions for two years, to hold the country for the Queen while he returned to England.

In the year 1587, Sir Walter Raleigh organized another colonial expedition consisting of 150 persons. This group included women and children—evidence of the true colonizing character of the project. Planters who signed on for the expedition were to receive five hundred acres of land and up in the New World. The whole thing was less military in nature than the earlier projects, and more of a genuine colonial expedition. Governor John White, who had been the artist of the first colony, was in charge.

Three ships left Plymouth on May 8 with this group and their possessions and supplies. There were persons on board who had been out on the earlier expeditions, and this gave continuity with the earlier attempts.

But when the colonists reached Roanoke Island, the fifteen men left there by Grenville were gone. The bones of one, apparently killed by Indians, were found. The fort had been razed, the houses were overgrown with vines, and hope of ever finding the men quickly vanished.

The season was late; so Governor White and his men began to dig in for the fall and winter ahead. The fort was rebuilt, the homes were repaired, and new cottages erected. The Indians were more hostile than ever, and many difficulties faced the sturdy band from England.

In this setting and amid these circumstances, on August 18, 1587, Governor White's daughter Eleanor, wife of Ananias Dare, gave birth to a daughter. She was named Virginia because she was the first child of English parentage to be born in the New World. Another child was born to Dyonis and Margery Harvie shortly afterwards. And on the earnest entreaty of the planters and colonists, Governor White sailed homeward on August 27, nine days after his granddaughter's birth, taking the fleet with him to get supplies for the colony.

With Governor White's departure on August 27, 1587, the history of events in the Roanoke Island colony became a tragic mystery which the generations since have vainly sought to explain. There had been talk of moving the colony fifty miles inland, and White had arranged for appropriate indications of their whereabouts if they removed from Roanoke Island before his return.

But because of England's war with Spain, which broke out meantime, White could not return as soon as he expected. A new fleet, that was to have gone to Virginia, was ordered into service against the Spanish Armada. The men concerned with Virginia were assigned tasks connected with England's defense, and no one could give more than thought to the colony on Roanoke Island.

At length the Queen's Privy Council gave permission to use two small ships not required for service against Spain, and White sailed with these on April 28, 1588. But the ships were small, poorly equipped, and inadequately provisioned. Partly because of these circumstances and partly because of their running after Spanish treasure ships, these ships were unable to reach America.

So while Grenville's larger ships contributed to the defeat of the Armada, the Roanoke Island colony was doomed for the lack of them. And although the Armada was defeated in the summer of 1588, the Anglo-Spanish battle of the Atlantic continued for several years. Meanwhile Raleigh deeded his interest in the New World enterprise to a group of London merchants and adventurers—including Governor White and nine others then on Roanoke Island—on March 7, 1589. One of the nine was Ananias Dare, father of Virginia Dare.

The months slipped by, months that must have been maddening for Governor White, who thought of his daughter and granddaughter, and the others, on Roanoke Island, perhaps suffering for supplies, perhaps embroiled in bitter warfare with the Indians. But the London merchants who had purchased the enterprise seemed unable to get a fleet organized for the relief and strengthening of the colony.

Finally, on March 20, 1591, Governor White sailed for America, but without supplies or newly recruited planters. In fact he was little more than a passenger on another's ship. After nearly five months of operating in the West Indies, this expedition, headed by Master John Wattes of London, finally anchored toward the evening of August 15 just off

Roanoke Island. Smoke was seen rising from the island, and that must have strengthened the sagging hopes of John White. On the following morning, August 16, Governor White and a small company set forth in two boats for the island. En route they saw another column of smoke rising to the southwest. This seemed to come from the general area occupied today by the Nags Head dunes. They decided to investigate this latter smoke column first. It was a wearisome task and consumed the whole day and led to nothing, since no human beings were at the scene of the woods fire.

The next day, August 17, they prepared to go to Roanoke Island. The party put off again in two boats. One of these capsized in a treacherous inlet and seven men were drowned. A fresh start was made; but before they could reach the place of settlement, it was so dark that they overshot their mark by a quarter of a mile. On the north end of the island they saw a light and rowed toward it. Anchoring opposite it in the darkness, they blew a trumpet and sang English songs, but received no answer. In the morning they landed but found only grass and rotten trees burning. From here they made their way to that part of the island where the colony had been left by Governor White. On this long trek along the shore they saw nothing of interest except a few footprints which two or three natives had made in the sand during the night.

And then they climbed a sandy bank that gave them their first view of the settlement they had left four years before.

A great change had taken place. The houses had been torn down and the area strongly enclosed with a palisade of tree trunks. As they drew nearer they saw that one of the chief trees in this fort-like arrangement had been peeled of bark, and carved in the bare wood was the single word: CROATOAN!

And all about was a great and oppressive silence. Not a single colonist remained. Not a sound or a sign or a communication—other than the one word cut in a tree. Just the wind from the ocean, the birds in the trees, and a great void where men, women, and children had been left four years before.

With the carved word there was no Maltese cross or sign of distress in accordance with the agreement made when White sailed for England. Things were thrown about inside the palisade and these were so overgrown with grass and vines that it was obvious the place had been abandoned for some time.

Governor White and his party then turned to the little bay which had been fortified with small ordnance and where the colony's small boats had been anchored. But there was no sign of these things. White next searched for certain chests and personal effects which he had secretly buried in 1587. But apparently the Indians had discovered the hiding place, because the chests were rifled, covers had been torn from books, and valuable maps and pictures had been spoiled by the weather.

But according to Governor John White's own words, in later reports on the occasion, he was cheered by the token word carved on the tree and had high hope that his daughter and her family, including granddaughter Virginia Dare, would be found on Croatan Island. The Indian, Manteo, who had been taken to England, was born on Croatan Island and the Indians there were friendly to the English.

Stormy weather was brewing; so White and his little group

returned in haste to the harbor where the ships were at anchor. The master of the ship agreed to go to Croatan Island the next day to look for the colonists. But when daylight came, the weather would not permit it. Instead, the ships were taken to the West Indies for fresh water, with plans to return to Croatan. But the elements willed otherwise, and the little fleet was blown toward the Azores, and from there finally limped home to England.

Governor White could not finance another expedition to America himself, and Raleigh also lacked the prince's purse that would have been required. White accepted the facts with resignation. His last recorded words, dated February 4, 1593, said that he left off from prosecuting the search not at his own will and added that he wished to God that his wealth were answerable to his will so that he could go on with the hunt.

However, as late as 1602 Raleigh was still seeking for his lost colony through other expeditions that traded with Indians along the coast. These parties apparently never engaged in very diligent searches because their reports frequently spoke of bad weather and unsafe conditions. Even after Jamestown was settled in 1607, the Virginia colonists inquired of the Indians about the lost colony of Roanoke Island, which by this time had become an imperishable English tradition. But hearsay reports were never sufficiently concrete to be of any real assistance in tracing the group.

So this first effort to colonize America ended in some kind of stark tragedy for those who were mysteriously swallowed up in the New World. And their fate—and the fate of little Virginia Dare, first white child born in America—remains a mystery to this day.

The Legend of Theodosia Burr

FOR this story we turn again to the state's picturesque Outer Banks, those narrow strips of sand that form the eastern boundary of the state, separating the ocean from the sounds. The early Indians called these banks "out islands."

Many legends have sprung from this treacherous stretch of the Atlantic coast, dotted with the wrecks of old ships, but the legend of Theodosia Burr is the favorite legend of the Carolina dune country. It has to do with a ghost ship that floated into port in 1812 with no life aboard—bringing with it mysteries that have not yet reached a positive solution.

One portion of one account of our story was written in 1869 by a Nags Head woman, who said:

"One bleak, December morning when leaden clouds dipped into an oily sea off Nags Head, there drifted ashore a small pilot boat with all her sails set and her rudder lashed. The craft, which was moving lazily with the tide, was apparently in good condition and aroused the curiosity of those who watched with sharp eyes from the sand dunes, ever alert for spoils from the sea. They fetched out their small boats and reached the drifting pilot boat. A hail after the manner of those who live by the sea brought no answer. Silence greeted the investigating party, a mysterious brooding silence that gave rise to superstitious awe, as they drew nearer the craft.

"Some of the bolder ones, armed to the teeth, boarded the pilot cautiously, alert for hidden danger or for signs of some dread plague. They found the ship entirely deserted. A table in one of the cabins had been set for a meal and remained undisturbed. There was no treasure in the way of gold or even silver, but on the wall of another cabin hung a beautiful portrait, and on a table were an intricately carved nautilus shell and a vase of wax flowers. There were also a number of handsome silk dresses cut in the empire style of long ago."

When the spoils of the deserted ship were divided, the dresses, flowers, shawls, and portrait fell to John Tillett, one of the wreckers. These treasures he presented to his sweetheart, who later became Mrs. John Tillett. John Tillett died and his widow married a Mr. Mann, who also died.

Mrs. Mann was left poor. The shack into which she was forced to move was constructed of driftwood and crude timber, unplastered, and fitted inside with home-made furniture. She peddled grapes for a living—grapes that have grown in great abundance in that country since before the days of Sir Walter Raleigh's Lost Colony. And then one day in 1869, fifty-seven years after the painting came to the island, Mrs. Mann became ill and called in Dr. William G. Pool, an Elizabeth City physician who summered at Nags Head. He visited the old woman in the Nags Head woods, driving a horse hitched to a cart, the customary mode of travel there at the time.

Seeing that Dr. Pool admired the painting and being without funds to pay him for his medical care and attention, Mrs. Mann gave it to him. Dr. Pool, conscious of its beauty and quite unaware of its identity or origin, took it back to his summer home at Nags Head, where it hung on the wall for over a decade.

So it was that the portrait of a beautiful young woman, quite unknown to anyone on the Banks, was shifted from the wall of a rude hut where it had hung for years to the possession of the physician.

It was an oil painting, on polished mahogany, twenty inches long, in a frame that was heavily gilded. The face in the painting was patrician and refined; the expression of the dark eyes proud and haughty; the hair dark auburn, curling and abundant. A white bodice, cut low in the neck and richly adorned with lace, revealed a glimpse of the drooping shoulders, and a snowy bosom. Years passed and during that time the portrait was the beautiful but rather meaningless possession of Dr. Pool.

Then an artist, who was in that region on a summer trip, chanced to see the painting. He examined it with care and interest and pronounced it first-class art indeed. In fact, the artist declared the painting a masterpiece and said it was unmistakably the portrait of some woman of aristocratic descent.

Some years later an old magazine chanced to fall into Dr. Pool's hands, and in it was an article on the tragedies of the household of Aaron Burr—including a sea voyage from Georgetown to the north. Dr. Pool read this article with attention, and from it learned the following story:

Aaron Burr had a daughter named Theodosia on whom he lavished his love and his wealth. Her great beauty, charm, dignity, and many accomplishments made her the toast of New York, Baltimore, and Philadelphia society and won for her the heart of Joseph Alston, one of South Carolina's early governors. She was married when she was eighteen years old.

The story of Theodosia Burr is perhaps one of the most tragic chapters in early American history. Her father, Aaron Burr, was once vice president of the United States and ranked among America's foremost statesmen. It was this same Aaron Burr who, after killing Alexander Hamilton in a duel, later schemed with Blennerhassett to colonize the territory west of the Mississippi River in preparation for a war with Spain— an activity which led to charges of treason.

Discredited by the Republican Party and later tried for treason at Richmond, Virginia, but acquitted, Burr spent four years in poverty and exile in Europe. Theodosia and her husband, Governor Alston, had been largely instrumental in making possible Aaron Burr's return to America in 1812. Thousands admired the daughter's heroic devotion to her father in the dark days of his disgrace and banishment.

Because of Burr's great unpopularity at this time, Theodosia took passage on a small and inconspicuous schooner bound from Georgetown, South Carolina, to New York, on which she and her party were the only passengers. Her one son, Aaron Burr Alston, had died a short time before.

It was on December 31, 1812, that the beautiful and universally admired Theodosia Burr Alston sailed aboard the small pilot boat, the *Patriot,* from Georgetown with her maid, her physician, and baggage, which included the portrait of herself.

Late into the night Dr. Pool read the article in the old magazine. It was accompanied by illustrations. Among other pictures was one of Theodosia Burr. The physician was struck by the likeness between the girl in the magazine and the girl in the oil painting that had come from the hut by the sea and had then hung on his own wall for a dozen years. He quickly convinced himself that the oil painting was a portrait of Theodosia Burr. He recalled the story of how the painting had made its way finally to the fishing shack where he had found it, and he was sure that the ghost ship which put in on the North Carolina coast was the *Patriot,* the ship in which Theodosia Burr had left Georgetown, sailing for New York and a reunion with her father after their long and tragic years of separation.

During the fifty-seven years the "Nags Head picture" of Theodosia Burr hung in old Mrs. Polly Mann's cabin back in the Nags Head woods, only an occasional stranger paid much attention to it. And strangers were few and far between in those days. The portrait of the beautiful woman hanging on the wall of old Mrs. Mann's bedroom must have looked strangely out of place there among her simple furnishings. Dr. Pool was fascinated by the dark and haughty beauty whose strangely-penetrating, jet-black eyes looked down from the portrait.

The magazine article on the Aaron Burr family and its parade of tragedies so convinced Dr. Pool that the picture in his possession was a portrait of Theodosia Burr Alston that he mailed photographs of the painting to members of the Burr and Edwards families. A reply came back:

"We identify the portrait as a likeness of Theodosia Burr Alston, who sailed to her death in a little pilot boat from Georgetown on December 30, 1812."

Additional proof came from Charles Burr Todd and Mrs. Stella Drake Knappin, of Michigan, descendants of the Burr and Edwards families, who eventually visited Dr. Pool's home on the coast.

Dr. Pool also carried a photograph of the painting to Washington and showed it to Colonel John H. Wheeler, author of *Historical Sketches of North Carolina*. Mrs. Wheeler, daughter of Thomas Sully, a famous painter who once painted Queen Victoria, spoke up:

"It is strikingly like one I have in my possession; let me show you."

The likeness of Theodosia Burr produced by Mrs. Wheeler compared identically with Dr. Pool's picture.

There were other vague links to hold the legendary story together. Two criminals about to be executed at Norfolk, Virginia, confessed to having been members of a pirate band that captured and plundered the pilot ship *Patriot*. They said they caused all hands on the *Patriot* to walk the plank.

A dying mendicant in a Michigan almshouse said he was aboard the vessel on the night when the *Patriot* was captured and looted. Babbling incoherently, he told of the strange beauty and bravery of a single girl passenger pleading for her life and promising pardons to all buccaneers if they would spare the crew and passengers. Her entreaties failed, he mumbled, and she walked the plank with a steady tread.

And so goes this story from the Carolina coast country of deep and silenced mysteries, of shifting sand dunes, and restless winds.

In 1936 in Raleigh, Robert Macbeth, owner of the Macbeth Galleries of New York and also the owner of an original portrait of Theodosia Burr, told the North Carolina Art Society that he acquired the portrait of Theodosia Burr from Dr. William G. Pool, Pasquotank County physician, almost one hundred years after Theodosia Burr sailed from Georgetown to visit her father in New York. The picture was back in North Carolina then, for the first time in half a century, and was on exhibit during an annual meeting of the North Carolina Art Society.

From the night Theodosia Burr Alston sailed out of Georgetown harbor until this day nothing has been heard of her except the Nags Head picture. Was she drowned at sea off stormy Cape Hatteras? Was her vessel captured by pirates and turned adrift with all sails set and rudder slashed so that it came ashore after the beautiful passenger had been forced to walk the plank? No one will ever know. But the famous (and now almost priceless) "Nags Head picture," which hung for so many years unnoticed in the fisherman's cottage back among the woods and sand hills above Nags Head is the peg on which this interesting and unsolved North Carolina mystery is hung.

The Peter Stuart Ney Mystery

MORE than a century after his death a mighty conflict still rages over the remains of Peter Stuart Ney, the mysterious schoolmaster of Rowan County. Was he a supreme imposter or was he the renowned Marshal of France?

A great battle of words—books, pamphlets and articles—has been waged for years over this matter. It is strongly contended that the man who posed as Peter Stuart Ney, a well-educated and well-travelled schoolteacher, given sometimes to sessions with the wine bottle, was in reality Marshal Ney of France, who had escaped execution on the continent and fled to America and to a secluded old age in rural North Carolina.

Who this strange man was, where he came from, what great secrets he might have taken with him to his grave in the cemetery at old Third Creek Presbyterian Church near the little town of Cleveland, between Salisbury and Statesville, constitutes one of the most exciting and one of the most involved of all the unsolved mysteries of our Tar Heel state.

The grizzled old schoolmaster who is the central character in this mystery died on November 15, 1846. He went to the Rowan County area some years before his death. A whole school of Ney historians has sprung up and great sheaves of evidence are available as proof that Peter Stuart Ney was Napoleon's brilliant strategist in his European wars. An equally strong case can be and is made out to the contrary. There is small chance that the question will ever be settled to anybody's satisfaction.

In our story we take a positive rather than a negative turn and summarize the evidence tending to show that the unusual schoolteacher was none other than Marshal Ney—in hiding. An abundance of evidence, much of which is hard to refute, has been piled up in support of the Ney legend during the past hundred years.

The story briefly is this. A Frenchman of distinctive bearing, obvious education, and wide experience, came to the United States through the port at Charleston and made his way to the rural stretches of Rowan County in North Carolina, where he settled down to live in a country home to teach the children in the community.

Those who had contact with him knew him as a genius at mathematics, a fine swordsman, a great horseman, and one who made vague and strange declarations when he sometimes sipped long and deep at the cup which cheers. He had mysterious visitors—foreigners—on rare occasions. News of the death of Napoleon affected him visibly and profoundly. He almost collapsed, in fact, and changed his enthusiastic and hopeful statements that he would someday return to France to statements indicating a complete disappearance of that interest.

Finally, an old man, he died, and on his deathbed declared that he was in reality Bonaparte's own Marshal Michael Ney of France.

And it is contended by many able historians and students who have carefully studied the case that after the turn of events which led to the arrest of Marshal Ney and his eventual condemnation to death before a firing squad, he was saved from that death and assisted in an escape to the United States to finish out his years here.

Marshal Ney was a ranking Mason. Those who were charged with his execution were Masons and were also his own former followers across the bloody battlefields of Europe. These facts give rise to the contention that the man whom Napoleon referred to as "My brave Ney" was not executed in Paris. It is reasoned that the firing squad of hand-picked veterans of campaigns under Marshal Ney was equipped with blank cartridges; that Ney feigned death and was quickly spirited aboard a waiting American-bound ship; and that another body fills the grave in Paris today marked as that of Marshal Michael Ney.

Safely in America, the one-time proud Marshal of France secluded himself in rural North Carolina and made his living by teaching school. And in the area that was then Rowan

County and has since been divided into several counties, a once great soldier who escaped with his life left in his wake a great mass of evidence to bear out just that contention.

Peter Ney, who shifted continually, taught in an area that today comprises Mecklenburg, Rowan, Lincoln, Iredell, and Davie counties, and in South Carolina. He once participated in a parade at Columbia, South Carolina, at the invitation of the Palmetto Governor. While riding on horseback beside the Governor, he was recognized by a Charleston Frenchman who had migrated to America after Napoleon's defeat and the Bourbon restoration. "Look, Henry. The big man beside the Governor. He's Marshal Ney! I'd know him anywhere," the man shouted. When Ney heard that several other Frenchmen had reported they had seen Marshal Ney, he left town immediately. He often told intimate friends that the fear of Bourbon assassination made it necessary for him to be on the move continually. In another instance, Ney was recognized at Statesville by a German emigrant who had fought under him in Switzerland.

Peter Stuart Ney, the schoolmaster, was known to have an astounding knowledge of the Napoleonic wars. He even corrected textbooks and writings and made marginal notes taking issue with the early historians who wrote about that period. And in subsequent years his version has been established as the correct one.

Whether an imposter or a grand illusionist, Ney was a profound student of Napoleonic history and possessed an uncanny knowledge of the most minute details of the period's warfare, court intrigues, and political scrambles. He read thoroughly every book and pamphlet on the French Revolution and the Empire that could be obtained, though the number coming into Carolina's middle country during those years was far from large.

In virtually every book he wrote dozens of marginal notes, a practice which provoked the wrath of several librarians. In the first volume of Sir Walter Scott's *Life of Napoleon* he penned, "This book should be thrown in the fire." In Volume II he inscribed, "This book contains more falsehoods than facts. It is little more than an historical romance." Several of the notes accused Scott of distorting facts with reference to Ney's actions on particular occasions—his ordering of a charge, his dispatching of a courier, his executing Russian prisoners, his summoning of men to the front. Many of his notes corrected errors in early and hastily-thrown-together accounts of the wars—errors which were detected and eliminated in later editions, or omitted completely in more accurate accounts. All notes showed a knowledge of Marshal Ney's life and the Napoleonic wars which could hardly have been gained by someone not on the scene and not in the inner clique of the French command.

A number of the Ney-inscribed volumes are now locked like treasure in the vaults of the Davidson College Library. They are not, however, Davidson's only connection with the schoolmaster, for Peter Ney designed in the early 1830's the seal still in use by the college.

There was a woman in the story, too, adding romantic interest. She was Ida Saint Elme, a Hungarian actress and self-styled adventuress. She had loved Ney—"Red Peter" as his friends called him to his face and his soldiers behind his back.

When her beauty began to fade, Ida Saint Elme took up her pen, and in her lively first book—*Memoirs of a Contemporary*, "by Ida Saint Elme, Adventuress, Paris, 1828"—

you may read of her desperate love for Michael Ney. In the volume she tells of his first visit to her at her house on Babylon Street in Paris, and of how she followed him in man's clothes over half Europe. When his love for her cooled she set snares in high places and charmed many notable men, including Prince Talleyrand and even the Emperor himself. Yet all the while, she wrote, she continued to love Michael.

Ida Saint Elme says that when Ney was condemned to death after Waterloo, she planned a rescue, and watched from a cab when he faced the Royalist firing squad in Luxembourg Gardens. But her book gives no hint that her rescue plan succeeded and that Ney continued to live. The volume was published thirteen years after the execution and—although it may have been a blind—the author mourned Ney as dead.

When Peter Ney drank too much, he talked in a muddle of French and English and on several occasions drew himself up to his full height to declare to closer friends and drinking companions that he was Marshal Ney of France. On his deathbed he told the physician who was attending him, and Osborne Foard in whose home he lived and died, that he was in truth Marshal Ney, described by Napoleon as his "bravest of the brave."

Behind the house where Peter Stuart Ney boarded in Rowan County was a stackyard where hay and straw were stored. On several occasions Frenchmen came to visit the schoolteacher, and they went out into the stackyard and talked there, sometimes staying all night.

In the rural countrysides where Ney taught he won instant respect. The people there knew at once that he was no ordinary country schoolmaster. They looked on him as the greatest man who had ever lived in their community and held to this conviction despite his one real weakness—the bottle.

He was in his classroom when the news of Napoleon's death at St. Helena reached him through a newspaper brought to school by one of the pupils. He fell instantly in a dead faint on the floor and that night tried to kill himself with a knife, which fortunately broke. Although he recovered physically, his spirit never mended. His hope had apparently been that the Bonapartist dynasty would be restored, so that he could return to his beloved France, his family, and his friends. But now his hope of an early return was shattered. And in his disappointment more and more he drank too much. And, sometimes, when he drank he talked.

On one occasion when he said—while in his cups—that he was Marshal Ney of France, he added that after he had been condemned to death a plan had been arranged to rescue him, and that the Duke of Wellington himself had made the success of the plan possible. He told how soldiers detailed to kill him were veterans of his old command, who were instructed to fire over his head. He added that he had been given a small sack containing liquid that was red and resembled blood. This he had under his shirt front. When he himself gave the command to fire, he lifted his hand high in a salute and then struck his breast as if to indicate where the aim should be. With that blow on his chest, he burst the sack so that the red liquid spurted all over his upper body and made a crimson spot on the ground when he threw himself down.

He was taken up, moved to a near-by hospital, and disguised. That night, after a farewell visit to his wife, he rode toward the coast. Finally reaching Bordeaux, he boarded a ship bound for America. He said that once during the voyage that followed he was recognized by a seaman who had formerly served under him in the army.

At first he told this story only on those occasions when he was a little drunk. Later he told the story when perfectly sober to men in the neighborhood who had become his intimate friends. He also related to them many of his experiences in the field, while aiding with the direction of the Napoleonic campaigns.

During the seven-year period that I newspapered at Salisbury near the heart of the locale of the Ney legend and a few miles from the Ney grave, I once examined a book that was the property of Alfred Buerbaum, the son of an old book dealer there and himself a book merchant. This book was one that had belonged to Peter Ney. It is a dictionary of quotations from many languages translated into English and published in Philadelphia in 1824. In the back of this book is a fine pencil drawing of a bust of Napoleon, presumably the work of the old schoolteacher. And then worked into the background of this picture, and in the same pencil strokes, using some of the same marks that outline the head of Napoleon, are smaller pictures of Napoleon's marshals, shown surrounding their chief. Each of the marshals in that drawing has a separate individuality.

Why should this strange and lonely old man be sketching Napoleon and his marshals in the back of a textbook as he heard the lessons of his students? Why did he not sketch George Washington or some other famous figure who might have appealed to a North Carolina schoolteacher of that day and age?

As he was about to die, Peter Stuart Ney said to those at his bedside, "The Old Guard is defeated. Now let me die."

Marshal Ney had led the Old Guard to victory and they went down together in defeat at Waterloo.

Before going on to the next item in our story, let me mention here the fact that Peter Ney devised his own system of shorthand which he taught to his Rowan pupils and in which he made vast numbers of notes and prepared elaborate manuscripts.

At Salisbury I also examined some home-made textbooks that once belonged to Wesley George and at the time were the property of his grandson, A. W. George. Wesley George was a student of Lucius Butler and Butler was Peter Ney's most gifted pupil. One of the textbooks is a shorthand textbook and is in the Ney system of shorthand—the same that was used for much of the old teacher's mysterious jottings and notes. Butler read this shorthand freely.

It is an accepted fact with the Ney historians that the old teacher had a mysterious trunk in his room, containing documents and papers that he guarded closely. Once when Ney was sick, Lucius Butler, the prize student, was in the teacher's room with him. Ney pointed to the old trunk and said, "In that trunk are papers that will shock and surprise the world. You are the only one who can read them all. When I am dead I want you to have them."

Upon receipt of the news of Ney's death, Butler set out immediately from his home to claim the trunk of the strange schoolmaster from overseas. But legend says that when he arrived at the Foard home where Ney lived and died, he found that the trunk had already been removed. Two men from Philadelphia had suddenly appeared and taken possession of it, departing as mysteriously as they had arrived.

The supporters of the Marshal Ney theory base many of

their claims on notarized statements by his former pupils, the last of whom died in 1927.

And now let us summarize the evidence favoring the fact that Peter Stuart Ney and Marshal Ney of France were one and the same. There is great similarity and much to be found in common in the physique, features, attitudes, qualities, skills, handwriting, and information possessed by Peter Stuart Ney the schoolmaster and Michael Ney the Marshal of France.

Great similarity between the two has also been found in mind, character, disposition, manners, habits, tastes, and temperament. As to the physical resemblance between Marshal Ney and Peter Ney, both were five feet and eleven inches tall, broad of shoulder, full chested, and well-muscled. Both had florid complexions and hair ranging between auburn and red.

The body of Peter Stuart Ney was scarred with old wounds. These corresponded to the wounds which Marshal Ney was known to have had. In every physical feature the published descriptions of Marshal Ney described Peter Stuart Ney also. Marshal Ney had been one of the best swordsmen in Europe, and the schoolmaster of Third Creek was an expert fencer.

Both were painstaking and methodical, impulsive and quick-tempered. Both had considerable personal magnetism.

Both Marshal Ney and Peter Ney used tobacco and drank spirits. Both *worshipped* Napoleon. Marshal Ney was a follower of Napoleon, and Peter Ney—an avid reader of the Napoleonic campaigns—made those mysterious corrections and marginal notes that in the light of later corrections in history proved to be dead right to an uncanny degree.

Both men existed on simple food and neither needed much

rest. Both have been described as having "souls of fire" and "frames of iron." Both were fair musicians. Both drew and painted with considerable merit. Both rode fiery horses with ease and grace. Both were past masters in the arts of warfare. Both tried a hand at poetry.

In the Napoleonic wars, Marshal Ney was wounded several times—in the foot, knee, thigh, hand, arm, chest, and neck. Peter Ney bore wounds in these same exact places on his body. When he was drinking wine, Peter Ney once told witnesses in Rowan County that he received certain hurts in the battle of Waterloo and he wrote a highly descriptive poem on the battle.

Both were well educated and spoke French and English fluently. Both were particularly adept in the fields of higher mathematics.

As to the matter of names, the French soldiers called Marshal Ney "The Red Lion" and "Red Peter" or "Peter the Red." It is argued that he might very naturally take on the nickname as a real name while in seclusion here in America.

Peter Stuart Ney came from France where Marshal Ney won his fame and suffered defeat.

Several handwriting experts have examined known samples of the writings of both men and have declared that both specimens came from a pen that was held in the same hand.

The ages of the two men coincide.

Probably the most important single piece of evidence supporting the claim was supplied by Peter Ney himself in a death-bed statement. Only an hour or so before the teacher died, his physician and friend, Matthew Locke, asked from the bedside: "Mr. Ney, there is something that has been puzzling us for years. Now we want to have the truth from

you. We want to know who you are." Raising himself upon
a pillow and looking Locke squarely in the face, Ney is quoted
by all of the three persons present as saying, "I will not die
with a lie on my lips. I am Marshal Ney of France."

The old teacher wrote in an album for one of his Rowan
neighbors and school patrons a poem that contained this
verse:

> Though I of the chosen the choicest
> To fame gave her loftiest tone,
> Though I 'mong the brave was the bravest
> My plume and my baton are gone.

Was that written by the military genius whom Napoleon
called his "bravest of the brave," just as the mysterious old
man expressed it in his poem?

If you are too much of a realist you may spurn the legend.
If you are romantically inclined you will be likely to de-
fend it.

The Odd Disappearance of a Sea Hero

FOR this story we turn back the pages of history to that time when our country was young and our Navy an infant—but an infant destined to grow into the sea power it is today. The hero of this story is a young man who played an exciting role in the early development of the United States Navy. His name, Captain Johnston Blakeley of Chatham County.

Blakeley lived and fought and sailed the seas in a day when victory in a sea battle was determined by the daring and courage of individual seamen rather than by the size and number of ships. Captain Johnston Blakeley achieved many glorious victories during the War of 1812, for daring and courage were certainly a prominent part of his character and make-up. The victory of his ship, the *Wasp,* over the English brig-sloop, the *Reindeer,* was one of the important naval engagements of that conflict.

The Chatham County man's rise to fame was not an accident. It was achieved by hard work, experience, and diligent study under teachers who had learned their lessons as heroes themselves during the naval warfare of the American Revolution. Captain Blakeley was a commander of skill and prudence. He was born at Seaforth, County Down, Ireland, in October, 1791. His father, John Blakeley, decided to bring his wife and family to America in 1782, and the little group set out across the Atlantic. Mrs. Blakeley and an infant son died at sea just before the ship docked at the South Carolina port of Charleston. The father and his motherless son, young Johnston Blakeley, remained in Charleston for about a year and then moved to Wilmington, where the father engaged in the mercantile business. While at Wilmington they became acquainted with Edward Jones, a fellow countryman and a descendant of Jeremy Taylor, eminent English bishop and author.

This meeting with Jones, who later became a solicitor-general here in North Carolina, proved to be a turning point in the life of young Blakeley. Jones took an instant liking to the young man and treated him like a son.

Jones had a magnificent colonial estate in Chatham County, a few miles northeast of Pittsboro, known as "Rock Rest." It was there that young Blakeley spent some of the more formative years of his young life. Meantime the father, John Blakeley, was doing well in his business at Wilmington.

With a portion of his growing fortune, he sent young Johnston to school at Flatbush in New York, to prepare him for entrance into the University of North Carolina at Chapel Hill. In 1796 the father died just before the son was to enter the University. It was natural that Edward Jones should be made executor of the elder Blakeley's estate and guardian of the son. From then on "Rock Rest" was young Blakeley's home and the associations there played an important part in the moulding of his character. Mrs. Jones, the former Mary Curtis Mallett, was like a mother to him. The Jones children, three daughters—later to be known as Mrs. Abram Rencher, wife of the territorial governor of New Mexico and ambassador to Portugal, Mrs. William Hooper, and Mrs. William Hardin, and one son, Dr. Johnston Blakeley Jones of Chapel Hill and Charlotte—all had brilliant careers.

Young Blakeley entered the University in 1797. His interests quickly turned to mathematics, navigation, and surveying. His leadership on the campus was demonstrated in his election as president of the Philanthropic Society, an important student organization of the day. His University career was cut short when a fire at Wilmington destroyed most of the property his father had left him and virtually wiped out his small fortune. His guardian insisted on paying the further expenses at Chapel Hill but Blakeley refused and on March 15, 1800, joined the United States Navy as a midshipman. Six years before that, on March 27, 1794, Congress had taken steps to give the United States some semblance of a real Navy. Depredations committed on our commerce by the piratical corsairs of the Barbary powers had forced the issue. The same Congress had ordered the building of four ships of 44 guns each and two of 36 guns each. John Adams, President of the

United States from 1797 until 1801, was a staunch advocate of an efficient Navy and pushed the matter with all his influence.

In May, 1800, when young Blakeley entered the Navy, it had only about thirty ships in service. He was assigned to a frigate, the *President,* flagship of Commodore Richard Dale in the Mediterranean, a 44-gun vessel. Commodore Dale was a remarkable old seaman who had served as a lieutenant on the gallant *Bonhomme Richard* of Revolutionary fame, where he was a favorite of John Paul Jones. Midshipman Blakeley sailed with Commodore Dale to the almost forgotten war with Tripoli.

Two years later Blakeley was ordered to the *John Adams,* a 31-gun ship under the command of Captain John Rogers, where he gained even more experience in a continuing war against the pirates of Tripoli. Then he served under Captain Rogers on the *Congress,* a brig with 36 guns that was later under the command of Commodore Stephen Decatur. When the Barbary powers declared that they had enough of Yankee warfare, Blakeley returned from the Mediterranean aboard the *President.*

Continuing his valuable experience with distinguished officers, he was assigned to the *Hornet* in 1805 under Lieutenant S. Evans, and later to the *Argus,* under Captain Jacob Jones, for a tour of duty along the Atlantic coast in 1806. He was commissioned a lieutenant February 10, 1807, and soon thereafter, on a furlough, his last one, visited "Rock Rest" and stopped off at Chapel Hill to see friends.

After this visit, Mrs. Charlotte Hardin, daughter of Edward Jones, described Lieutenant Blakeley in words as follows: "His face was handsome and kindly; his eyes black

and sparkling, his teeth when displayed by his frequent win-
ning smiles, of exceeding whiteness. His hair was coal black
in youth, but even at the age of 26, turning rapidly gray. His
person was small but strong and active, and his motions easy
and graceful. He was grave and gentlemanly in his deport-
ment, but at the same time, cheerful and easy when at home;
among strangers rather reserved."

During the next two years Lieutenant Blakeley saw service
at the Norfolk Navy Yard. Then he was attached for a time
to the *Essex,* and then again to the *John Adams.* He was given
his first command on March 4, 1811, when he was placed in
charge of the *Enterprise.* He handled this ship so well that on
July 24, he was commissioned a master commandant.

Then came trouble with Great Britain. In the early stages
of this difficulty, Blakeley felt strongly that the United States
was making a mistake in assuming the role of pacifist and felt
that the course was proper when Congress made a formal
declaration of war against Great Britain on June 18, 1812.

As the war of 1812 got underway, Great Britain had 800
effective ships. The United States had 17 cruisers that could
be classed as effective. But Blakeley was elated nonetheless. His
first task was to direct the remodeling of the *Enterprise,* a
14-gun brig. This done, he sailed with her and roamed the
Atlantic coast, relentlessly searching for British privateers.

On August 20, 1813, he captured the privateer schooner,
the *Fly,* and on that same day was placed in command of a
new ship, the *Wasp.*

The *Wasp* was being built to replace another ship of the
same name, a ship commanded by Captain Jacob Jones, which
had captured the British *Frolic* and in turn was taken by another British warship. The new *Wasp* was constructed at

Portsmouth, New Hampshire, and several months were required to equip her and train the crew. But Blakeley was a master at handling men. His crews were often described as the finest that ever sailed the seas.

During this brief interlude, romance crept into Blakeley's life. While the *Wasp* was being made ready, he found time to journey on occasions to Boston, where he won the heart of a beautiful girl, Jane Ann Hooper. She was the daughter of a New York merchant who had been a friend of his late father in his days as a Wilmington merchant. They were married. But war begrudges time for love, and a few months later, on May 1, 1814, Blakeley set sail with the *Wasp*— never to return.

The *Wasp* was just what her name implies. An 18-gun ship with a crew of 173 officers and men, mostly New Englanders and veterans of war with the British, French, Spanish, and Malay pirates, she set her sails toward the western entrance of the English Channel in search of ships of the British merchant marine. Instead of commerce ships, Blakeley ran first into a British warship, the brig-sloop *Reindeer,* under the command of one of England's most gallant seamen of all time, Captain William Manners, a scion of the ducal house of Rutland.

At first it seemed as if the *Reindeer* had the advantage, for she fired her 12-pound shifting carronade five times at a distance of sixty yards before the *Wasp* could get into position to retaliate. The *Reindeer* also mounted sixteen 24-pound carronades and two long 9-pounder guns. Blakeley finally brought the *Wasp* into position and in exactly nineteen minutes had literally cut the *Reindeer* to pieces. Manners, the English Captain, though shot through both thighs, was still shouting orders when a shot pierced his brain and brought him down. The Americans boarded the ship and made the crew prisoners. On the *Reindeer* thirty-three were killed, thirty-four wounded, while the *Wasp* counted eleven killed and fifteen wounded. The *Reindeer* was so badly damaged that Blakeley found it necessary to burn the ship after the crew had been removed. Taking no credit for himself, Blakeley was high in the praise of his crew after the encounter.

On July 8, the *Wasp* put into L'Orient, France, for repairs, after capturing an additional number of prizes. She remained there until August 27, when she again spread her sails before the wind. It was September 1 when she fell in with the British sloop of war, *Avon*, of 20 guns, commanded by Captain Arbuthnot. After an action of forty-five minutes, the *Avon* was compelled to surrender, her crew being nearly all killed or wounded. The *Wasp* listed two killed and one wounded. Other British ships of war, of vastly superior force, approached the scene and the *Wasp* was forced to retire.

Blakeley continued his cruise, creating great havoc among English merchant vessels and privateers, and from May 1 to September 30, 1814, the *Wasp* captured a total of 15 vessels.

By now the *Wasp*, Captain Blakeley, and his crew must have felt a little cocky over their record. The *Wasp* had stung many she had encountered and she had hung up a record in the then very young Navy of the United States that was the envy of the entire battle fleet. The *Wasp* had become a magic word meaning hard fighting at sea and success in those hard fights.

The *Wasp* sailed toward the southwest. On October 19, 1814, she spoke to the Swedish brig, *Adonis*. After exchanging courtesies, Captain Johnston Blakeley and the *Wasp* sailed on through the misty sea—on beyond the horizon—never to be seen or heard of again.

After that odd disappearance of ship and crew, various rumors spread. An English frigate, badly crippled, reported at Cadiz that it had a severe fight with a large American ship at night and that at the height of the battle, the American ship suddenly disappeared in the dark ocean. There was a report that the *Wasp* was wrecked on the African coast and that her crew became prisoners of the Arabs. Another story was that the *Wasp* reached the coast of South Carolina and on November 21 was attacked by an English frigate of superior strength, and although she beat off the British ship, she herself was sunk. Another story said the *Wasp* went down in a tornado, and still another report, that she was the victim of an accidental magazine explosion. None of these stories was ever confirmed.

In the period of conjecture and uncertainty over the fate of the *Wasp* and of Captain Blakeley and the crew, considerable attention and sympathy was directed to his wife, Jane, and their infant daughter, Maria Udney, who had been born in January, 1815. The State of North Carolina and the national government provided generously for the support of these two tragic figures.

Among other recognitions, the State of North Carolina presented Blakeley's widow with a silver service, out of appreciation for the Navy hero's bravery and service to his state and nation.

Mrs. Blakeley eventually married a Dr. Abbott of Christiansted, on the Isle of St. Croix, in the West Indies, a possession of Denmark. The daughter, Maria Udney, grew to womanhood and married Barron Joseph Von Bretton of the West Indies in 1841, and on March 2 of the following year died in childbirth at the age of twenty-seven. So the blood line of Johnston Blakeley became extinct.

The silver service presented to Mrs. Blakeley soon after her husband's disappearance showed up in North Carolina in the 1930's. An agent from London arrived in Raleigh with the silver, displayed it at the Capitol and at various points about the state, and the story of its connections and interests was told and retold.

And then it developed that the owners were offering it for sale. An effort was made to have the State of North Carolina purchase it, for its sentimental as well as historical value. This failed because a depression was on and public money like private funds was short and precious. Efforts to sell it to some person of means followed, but these also failed—largely because of the fabulous price that was asked, even after several reductions were offered from the first announced price. The agent finally packed up the silver and left. But that is merely a modern-day sidelight on the story.

The spirit of the hero, Johnston Blakeley still lives. It hovered over our infant Navy and has continued to challenge the men of the Navy to this day.

And that's the story of a Navy hero and the heritage he left when he and his *Wasp* disappeared so strangely at sea nearly a century and a half ago.

A Shepherd of the Hills

THIS is the story of the Reverend W. T. Hawkins, a "shepherd of the hills" who walked from his home in the beautiful Sapphire country of Western North Carolina into the twilight—and has never been seen or heard from to this day.

Many years have sped by, and the rugged Sapphire country still refuses to give up its secret. It was a March afternoon in 1930 and the sun had just set over Timber Ridge, which sprawls alongside Cashiers Valley. The Reverend W. T. Hawkins, a seventy-three-year-old retired Methodist minister, disappeared as if by some oriental magic, leaving behind him a mystery as deep as the silence of the high hills into which he walked that blustery afternoon.

Of course there were explanations, but they did not explain; solutions, but they did not hold. Not so much as a bleached bone or a rusty buckle has ever been found. The riddle of what became of the man known in the rugged area bordering the South Carolina line as something of a twentieth-century medicine man of the mountains is still unsolved.

It was about 5:30 in the afternoon, chilly as March is always chilly in the mountains. Dark was approaching, and the family cow, grazing somewhere on Timber Ridge, had not come in at lowing. The elderly minister buttoned up his coat and set out to find her, leaving his son-in-law, Joe Wright, roasting his shins before an open fire, and his daughter, Joe's wife, puttering among her pots and pans in preparation of supper.

Night, like day, comes suddenly in the hills. The perpetual ripples on Lake Cashiers became only sound as darkness inked them out. Supper, spread upon the table awaiting the old man's return, began to grow cold. The daughter was first impatient, then uneasy. Seven, then seven-thirty, came.

"Joe," the old minister's daughter said to her husband, "something has happened to Papa."

Joe Wright was not sure in his own mind, but he didn't want her to worry.

"He's likely down at the store," he said. "I'll go see."

The store was the center of the little village of maybe a dozen houses. Menfolk forgather there of evenings to talk and whittle, and little passes unnoticed. But Tom Hawkins was not there. Some of those present saw him leave toward Timber Ridge. None saw him return. No one gave the hoped-for answer that he had stopped in with some neighbor "to rest a spell."

Parson Hawkins had always walked and moved with vigor that belied his years. His friends and neighbors knew him as a strong and capable man, perfectly at home in the hill country he loved.

But these hills are as sinister as they are picturesque. Cashiers Valley drowses there in the hills today, as it did in 1930, beneath the precipitous Devil's Courthouse and the towering Whiteside Mountain, landmarks that are well known to those who frequent Western North Carolina. These places, bearing names that might have come fresh from a Sherlock Holmes story, had never held any fear, or even awe, for the aging minister. But as the daughter kept the supper waiting, his expected footstep was not heard on the porch. The little clock on the mantel of the Wright home ticked off the count as anxiety grew into alarm.

Then word began to be passed that Tom Hawkins was lost. A searching party was formed; and man and boy alike, carrying lanterns and flashlights, searched the face of Timber Ridge.

Dawn brought a cold rain, and the mountains became gray and foreboding. And gray and worn were the spirits of the searching party who had braved the dangers of Timber Ridge, which at one point breaks into a thousand-foot precipice. The searchers returned empty-handed. They had followed all of the precipitous trails that tunnel through undergrowth as they wind around Timber Ridge.

Three days later, citizens from near-by towns of Sylva, Brevard, Cullowhee, Glenville, Highlands, and places in South Carolina made up a party of some five hundred which dragged the hills of the Sapphire country, but they found no more than had the small group who had taken to the forest on the night of the disappearance.

The news spread, and others familiar with the Sapphire country took up the search. Again and again these groups plunged back into the wooded hills for hours of hunting and searching. Again and again they returned empty-handed. Over precipitous trails and along the foot of some of the more dangerous cliffs, the search continued. Yet the hunters knew that the missing man was so familiar with the country and such an expert woodsman that he could hardly have become lost there.

But though the Timber Ridge area was combed again and again for a trace of the missing man, not a single clue was ever found. Only an empty echo answered the frantic "hellos" that were hurled into the coves.

So the searching parties comprising crack woodsmen from the area came in from the tangled forest of Timber Ridge— one by one. Their clothes were torn and their eyes were swollen from strain and lack of sleep. Many of them came in from the ridge without a word. They knew that the search, which had continued in ever widening circles, had become futile.

After two weeks it was abandoned entirely. The minister was given up as dead. The searchers, rugged mountaineers, some of them with several days' growth of beard on their faces, went back to their homes to shake their heads sadly and to ponder the mystery.

Some said Tom Hawkins had fallen into Lake Cashiers. The lake was drained, but it yielded no corpse. Some said he had fallen over the Timber Ridge precipice and lay in some niche beyond the reach of man. But no tell-tale vultures were ever seen circling the cliff for carrion. Some said he had been whisked away in a car, killed and robbed, but that made little sense, for automobiles are rare in the hills into which Tom Hawkins went. The minister's family said that he had little or nothing of value on his person that might have tempted robbers.

Someone recalled that the Reverend Mr. Hawkins had accidentally come upon moonshiners and their illicit still a short time before when he was on one of his rambling hikes. Maybe these moonshiners had eliminated the witness to their manufacture of contraband. But those who knew the Parson best were not altogether convinced, for they were aware that, although he frowned upon whiskey and its manufacture, he would never have reported the information he had stumbled upon. The whole philosophy of his preaching and ministry had been proclaimed from his pulpit many times; he sought only to lead men to right living. He would never try to force them to righteousness—with the aid of the strong arm of the law. So that theory quickly melted away in the face of the community's knowledge of its "shepherd."

Again, those neighbors of the vanished minister say there is the possibility that he may have attempted to explore some unknown mountain cavern and been wedged between falling boulders. But it is highly unlikely that he would have started on such an expedition at dusk.

Even the remote possibility that he may have been attacked by some animal while lying helpless has been thoroughly examined.

Some credence was given to the suggestion that he may have attempted to capture a rattlesnake (a feat that had become his hobby over a long period of years) and had been fatally bitten. In an attempt to reach aid he may have staggered into the underbrush and died there. But many recalled that in the summer of 1929 he was bitten on the hand by a ferocious rattler at Cashiers as he was extracting the poison sac, just as he had done with so many other snakes before he again set them free. Bystanders rushed forward to kill the reptile then; but he smiled and waved them aside, pointing out that the snake had acted only as nature had intended and therefore did not deserve death. After treatment his hand healed, and within a few weeks he was capturing snakes again.

The possibility that he became ill, or broke a bone and could not reach assistance, was also taken into consideration. However, such an expert woodsman, hunter and fisherman was he that no one in the Sapphire country believes that he could become even momentarily confused as to direction to the nearest aid. The "shepherd of the hills" was known and loved by the entire section and could have called at any household and been in the hands of a friend.

Suggestion of suicide was bluntly brushed aside by those who knew W. T. Hawkins. He was of such cheerful temperament that it was hard to think of him as resorting to such an act of violence. Besides, they remind, he had no worries that anyone knew of, and he was in perfect health.

It is unlikely that Tom Hawkins, an experienced woodsman, became lost in the hills he had for years called home. It's hard to lose a mountain man in his own mountains, every peak of which he knows by name.

As the search came to an end, the minister's saddened little family centered its hope in the possibility that someone would some day happen upon the body and restore it to them to lay beside that of the wife and mother there in the little Cashiers Valley churchyard.

Then, without warning, the Wright home was one night enveloped in flames and destroyed. The family escaped but succeeded in saving few valuables. Some said the fire was of incendiary origin. This suspicion swept the community; and the belief gained headway that the same person, or persons, responsible for the fire, may have also murdered the aged minister. Joe Wright, the son-in-law, did not share this belief entirely, for he felt that since the blaze started in the kitchen, it may have been the result of carelessness in leaving fire in the stove. Fellow mountaineers pointed out that it is nothing unusual for the tinder-dry shingles of the average mountain home to ignite from a flying spark.

If the two incidents had any connection, clues to link them were never discovered.

After sixteen years of silence the consensus in the Sapphire country has crystallized into the belief that the minister may have fallen from one of the sheer precipices which drop for as much as a thousand feet, and that the body was so perfectly concealed in the dense undergrowth below that even sharp mountain eyes could not distinguish it even after prolonged search.

Those in Cashiers Valley most familiar with the topography of the section doubt that any remaining trace of the body will ever be found now. Yet there are those so devoted that these many years afterwards they still cling to the dream that the mortal remains will be restored some day by a chance discovery.

Only one thing about this case is definitely known: Tom

Hawkins walked away in the twilight never to return—and another chapter was added to the great unsolved.

Our beautiful North Carolina Sapphire country holds the shrouded secret of what happened to the lovable and friendly Parson Tom Hawkins, still remembered in Cashiers Valley for his kindly deeds and good work. His friends—his people—there in the mountains know that whether he be sleeping at the foot of a precipice of Timber Ridge, or in Whiteside Cove, or on the heights of a mountain range, it is all very likely just as he would have wished it. He lived with the trees and the shrubs, with the flowers and animals. It is doubtful that he would ask more of death. So if Tom Hawkins sleeps there in the Sapphire hills, his spirit knows much of the solace and consolation that he gave others in his lifelong role as a "shepherd of the hills."

The Brown Mountain Lights

IN THE majestic mountain country of Western North Carolina is the highest peak east of the Rockies. This well-known formation is Mount Mitchell in Yancey County. Western North Carolina also boasts of Clingman's Dome, Grandfather Mountain, Chimney Rock, Linville Gorge, Blowing Rock, Table Rock, and others. They are all widely publicized and well-known peaks, mountains, and formations.

But perhaps the most famous of all the Western North Carolina hills is up in Burke County, not far from Morganton. It is not a very high mountain; there is nothing remarkable about its formation; there are no sensational lines, peaks, or cliffs. It has, in fact, a rather commonplace name, in contrast to some of the more picturesque designations that have been given to certain points in the Land of the Sky.

This mountain is known as Brown Mountain. It isn't, in truth, much of a mountain as mountains go. It lies somewhat in the foothills of the Blue Ridge and is only 2,600 feet in elevation. But its fame lies in certain mysterious lights that have long hovered over it during the night.

These lights, known for many years as the Brown Mountain Lights, not only have attracted the attention of the people of this state but have aroused the curosity of a nation as well. In fact, this interest has been of such extent that two separate and formal investigations have been conducted by the United States Geological Survey.

The lights are extremely faithful and make their appearance with remarkable regularity—when the weather is such that the presence of the lights can be checked on. Sometimes they can be seen and sometimes they can't. But usually, in fair weather, not too much patience is required for a look at the bobbing lights.

Persons who wish to see the lights can take up their position at Wiseman's View on Highway No. 105 near Morganton, about eight o'clock in the evening and look to the southeast. The Linville-Grandfather Mountain area is also a vantage point. Suddenly there will appear a light about the size of a toy balloon. It is very red in color, and it will rise over the summit of the mountain, hover there momentarily, and then disappear.

In a few minutes, the light will appear again, but at another point on the mountain. And so, through the night, the lights appear, disappear, and then reappear, at different points around the mountain, but nowhere else.

As is the usual thing in such cases, the observers have never been quite able to agree on just what they see. To one observer the light is pale—almost white, is restricted to a definite circle, reappears several times in rapid succession and then fades out for twenty minutes, only to reappear in the same circle.

Another formal report, made by an observer several miles away from the first observer quoted, saw the light soon after sunset. It was a glowing ball of fire, he said, yellowish in color. It persisted for half a minute and then disappeared. To this man the light appeared as a bursting skyrocket, only much brighter.

To some the light seems stationary and to others it moves about in different directions.

A minister once wrote that the lights appear to him as an incandescent ball of fire. The theories advanced to account for the lights are many, varied, and sometimes as fantastic as the lights themselves. The superstitious see in them manifestations of the supernatural. Students of the earth and its formation have tried to explain the mystery through deposits of mineral ores. Boyish pranks have been considered— although it would have been a pretty long-drawn-out prank, or succession of pranks by succeeding pranksters.

But the lights have been so alluring that scientific minds have devoted hundreds of hours of study to the matter. Interested persons have spent months of time in contemplation. And reams of paper have been consumed in stories written and theories advanced. A great number of strange and uncanny stories have sprung from the existence of the lights.

Everybody who has seen them apparently has some theory about the Brown Mountain Lights.

Of course, it has been suggested that the strange light is a will-o'-the-wisp, but this theory does not hold because there are no bogs or marshes in the vicinity. Others suggest phosphorus, but that element oxidizes rapidly and is never found in the free state. Still others say that it is fox fire, but the light is too pale and feeble for this classification. It has been suggested that beds of pitchblende ore, from which radium is derived, are present in the vicinity. But even if this were true, there would be no light because the rays from radium are invisible. And, supposing radium rays were visible, they would give off a constant glow and not the intermittent and spasmodic gleam of the Brown Mountain Lights. However, the geologists have settled once and for all the matter of a possible geological explanation of the puzzle by announcing that Brown Mountain is composed of ordinary Cranberry granite, with no strange, weird, or interesting additions to that base.

Hydrogen sulphide and lead oxide were reported in the vicinity, and the lights have been attributed to this. Then there is the theory that moonshiners operate on the mountains, firing their stills on the distant hillsides at night. And, of course, it is quite likely that contraband has been made on those very hillsides. But this still doesn't explain the intermittent character of the lights as seen from vantage points at some distance away from the mountain.

St. Elmo's fire has been brought forward in explanation. This is an electrical discharge which accompanies a thunderstorm under certain atmospheric conditions, especially at sea. But since the lights appear when there is no storm and when the skies are clear, this theory, like many others, has had to be discarded.

Someone tried to apply the theory of the Andes Lights. This is a phenomenon of the high Andes, where silent discharges of electricity pass through the clouds to the mountain peaks. This discharge produces a light with a circular border that is visible at great distances. But the Andes Lights —so called—appear only at very high altitudes, some 15,000 feet or more. Brown Mountain is much too low in elevation for the Andes Light phenomenon to occur there.

Then the desert mirage theory was advanced. There was some reasoning that air currents of different densities and inequalities in temperature might produce reflecting surfaces from which the brighter stars could be reflected.

Carl A. Witherspoon, Jr., is one who sticks to the mirage explanation. He said of the Brown Mountain Lights that it is "not one of those things you *think* you see, but an actual transmission of light through heat layers acting as lens and prisms and projected on some barrier or mist or dust particles...."

William V. Dodge belongs to this same general school. He wrote that his grandmother, Emma J. Dodge, had a summer cottage at Linville Falls and that he had visited there often. "During practically every one of my visits there," he writes, "I made it a point to see the 'lights,' usually from Jonas Ridge, or Bald Ground, both of which are marvelous vantage points, and I have formed a conclusion. It is best explained by the seeming 'pool' of heat that every motorist has seen on a paved highway somewhere in front of him, which 'pool' reflects oncoming cars, etc. Now, it is my theory that every night, when the cool air comes down the valley from the higher mountains to the northwest, this cool air forces the warm valley air to rise, and as Brown Mountain is a long, low, flat ridge, it will move slowly over this ridge, reflecting stars, or any other light, by a distortion of the atmosphere.

"Most people will grant that it is a distortion of the atmosphere, but I think most of them try to visualize a light reflected from somewhere on the ground, but they strike a dead-end when they try to explain that the 'lights' were just as bright as ever after the great flood of 1916, when no lights were to be had on the ground. I can't ever recall having seen the Brown Mountain Lights when the sky was overcast, thus strengthening my conviction that the 'lights' are reflections of stars, caused by a distortion of the atmosphere which is in turn caused by warm valley air being forced over Brown Mountain by cold mountain air."

Dr. J. H. Brendell, a Methodist minister, first heard about the Brown Mountain Lights from his grandfather, who had said that the light rose up from the mountain something like a moon to remain suspended there in the air for a time and then fade out. When he was a veteran minister, Dr. Brendell was sent to the Table Rock charge of the Methodist Church near the heart of the Brown Mountain Lights country. His interest in the story his grandfather used to tell him was revived, and Dr. Brendell talked to many old and young people about the lights. From them he got the impression that the natives regarded newspaper accounts and attempted scientific explanations to be generally erroneous. No explanation was satisfactory to these people.

"Late one dark and sultry August night," Dr. Brendell wrote, "I came home with my family to the parsonage. We had been to a revival service. As we got out of the car, one of my sons looked toward the West in the direction of Brown Mountain and exclaimed, 'Look! There is the Brown Mountain Light.'

"We looked, and there was the light several feet above the mountain top. It looked to be larger than any star, was cone-shaped, and appeared to be something on fire. While we were looking, another one, not so large, came up from the eastern side and soon flickered out. Another came up from the western side and did the same way. We looked through a field glass, and found that it looked even more like a ball of flame. It slowly rose higher, growing smaller all the while, until it finally went out. . . ."

Dr. Brendell was seeing with his own eyes the thing that his grandfather had told him as a boy—how a light would rise from the mountain, suspend in air, and then fade out.

A physicist who went to the scene quickly hit on the theory that what was seen from Rattlesnake Knob was loco-motive headlights. But a headlight on a locomotive or an automobile would cast a beam of light, like a searchlight, and not a ball of light as this appeared to be.

Those hardest to satisfy with an explanation of the Brown Mountain Lights are the people who live in the vicinity and have grown up near the lights and in year-to-year association with them.

Early in 1947, J. L. Hartley, a veteran State Fire Warden from that mountain area, reduced to writing his theory that the lights are there by divine power. He said: "If God could make Brown Mountain, could he not also make the lights?" He added:

"I have lived for sixty years in sight of Brown Mountain.

From 1914 to 1922 I supplied the State Hospital at Morganton with beef cattle. This caused me to travel the old Jonas Ridge to Morganton at all times of the night. This road leads about two miles south of the base of Brown Mountain, and I have seen the lights looking north from this road.

"At that time for a distance of twenty miles looking north, this was a part of the Pisgah National Forest and a vast wilderness. No automobiles could travel there, and no voices were heard there save those of God and the Black bear.

"On Linville Mountain you have between you and Brown Mountain, looking north, Ginger Cake, Short Off, and Table Rock Mountains. This chain is much higher than the Wiseman's View outlook. Therefore it excludes any view of Brown Mountain. I have served as a State Fire Warden for thirty years and have fought forest fires on every mountain from Linville Falls to Blowing Rock at all times of the night, and have seen these lights a great many times from Grandfather Mountain above any human habitation. It is true there were hunters with lanterns, but please tell me whoever saw a lantern ascend up into the elements where no game exists. . . ."

This "divine power" explanation is typical of the feeling that residents of the mountain country have toward the phenomenon, oddity, reflection, illusion, or what-have-you.

Brown Mountain natives argue energetically that the scientists are all wrong. They like to recount the tale of a woman of that region who disappeared about 1850. There was a general suspicion in the area that the woman's husband had murdered her. Almost everyone in the community turned out to help search the mountainside for her body. One dark night while the search was on, strange lights appeared over Brown Mountain. These were not like any lights that anyone in the searching party had ever seen before. Some were scared and contended that the lights, bobbing away there, were in fact the spirit of the dead woman come back to haunt her murderer—and maybe to keep people from searching for her body.

The search ended without even a trace of the woman—unless possibly some blood stains found on a stile could be traced to her. The husband explained these stains by saying they came from a pig he had butchered a few days before and which he had carried across the fence by way of this stile.

A little while after that, a man who was relatively a newcomer to the neighborhood left the community with a fine horse and wagon that had belonged to the missing woman's husband. The husband said that the man had bought them, but everyone knew that the newcomer had shown no evidence of having money. He was never heard from again, but people assumed that he had either helped with the murder or had known of it and had been bribed to leave.

But the body was eventually found. Long years afterwards, a pile of human bones was found under a cliff. These were identified as the skeleton of the missing woman. This legend accounts for the first time that the Brown Mountain Lights are said to have appeared. They have been seen at intervals in all the years since—down to this day.

In 1922 a Federal Government geologist was assigned to make a survey and study of the Brown Mountain Lights phenomenon. He arrived in Burke County with a complete layout of scientific equipment for the job at hand. He had topographic maps, a plane table, telescopic equipment, a barometer, compasses, flashlights, camera, field glasses, and so on.

This man observed conditions and made a careful study extending over several weeks. With his maps spread out and his equipment mounted in place, he sighted landmarks, plotted lines, and worked with angles. In his final report, after making this careful survey, he said the Brown Mountain Lights came from a wide variety of things. He reported that 47 per cent of the lights were caused by automobile headlights, 33 per cent by locomotive headlights, 10 per cent came from fixed lights, and 10 per cent from brush fires.

It was this man's contention that, although the lights seem to hover over Brown Mountain, actually they originate beyond. Highway and rail traffic, homes or other fixed objects, some of them in the broad valley beyond the mountain, together with an occasional brush fire, supply the mysterious dancing lights over Brown Mountain.

These conclusions, complete with certain scientific data to back up each of them, were viewed with some disdain by older residents of the community. These residents said that the Brown Mountain Lights were visible before there was any railroad through Burke County or in that section of North Carolina. They were also visible before even the invention of the automobile, much less its use on non-existent highways in the mountains.

And then it was also pointed out that the lights had never been known to appear after a long dry spell. That blasted the brush fire part of the theory.

One native stood with his back to both the highway and the railroad, and in that position still witnessed the mysterious lights as they appeared above the mountain crest. To this he added a final convincing proof, which tends to render completely negative these findings. In 1916 during the great flood in Western North Carolina, trains and automobiles did not operate in that area for a week or more, but during that time the Brown Mountain Lights appeared as usual. Apparently some other solution must be sought.

And while an explanation satisfactory to all is a very will-o'-the-wisp itself, people still go there to look from Wiseman's View across to Brown Mountain. And when the conditions—whatever they may be—are just right, they see the dancing, flickering, mysterious Brown Mountain Lights that have baffled those who have seen them for many years.

Polly Williams, a Race Horse Mystery

~~~~~~

MOST of the unsolved mysteries treated in this collection have concerned incidents in which people have had a part. But now we vary the menu by presenting a story about a race horse.

Horses and horse racing have a definite and established place in the history of our state and of the South. Trials of speed and endurance between horses began centuries before the Christian era. Racing horses drew chariots, then lighter vehicles, and finally they carried only their riders.

The sport as we know it today had its rise in Britain under the reign of James I. It was later, in the reign of George II, in 1730, that the race horse made his appearance in America. Samuel Patton and George Grist brought the English horse, Bulle Rock, to this country to begin an era of horse races and of horses so great that they made their names felt in the early history of America.

The horse that Patton and Grist brought to this country well over two hundred years ago was landed in Virginia. The first race meetings in America took place in Virginia in 1753. The first regular American racing organization was formed that same year at Charleston, South Carolina, where the famous Washington Course was located.

The race courses of that day were the centers of social life. George Washington frequently acted as a judge at the races. By the time of the Revolution the breeding of race horses had progressed so far in this country that stud farms were in existence from the Carolinas to Long Island. During the Revolutionary War, this activity of course received little attention; but with the surrender of Cornwallis, the turf in this area began to flourish again. However it was not until 1815 that the race meetings of America were conducted on anything like systematic plans. Since that time authentic records have been regularly kept. Before that time the records are fugitive and do not present a full history of the American turf.

But reaching into that dim background we do have the authenticated story of the Polly Williams race horse mystery. The story is, of course, also about the people who owned and loved and raced Polly Williams; but that beautiful and graceful animal, a queen of the fast-steppers of the turf of her day, is the central character in this episode.

Polly Williams was a sorrel mare, foaled in the year 1774

in Dinwiddie County, Virginia. The expert judges of horse flesh in her day described Polly Williams as "very highly formed, with beautiful fore parts, and a very high goose rump, ragged hips and a very narrow behind." She had a large blazed face, and all four legs were white. She was bred by Peter Williams of Dinwiddie County and was descended from such fine racing stock as Lee's Old Mark Anthony, Old James, Old Janus, Old Fearnought, Jolly Roger, and an imported mare named Mary Gray.

This celebrated Polly Williams mare never produced a foal.

The story of Polly Williams has been handed down to present-day horse lovers from various sources in Virginia and North Carolina. Polly Williams, who early showed promise of exceptional speed and grace on the racing turf, came to be the property of William Davis of Warren County in North Carolina—"Old Mr. Davis" every written account of the Polly Williams story described him. The full name has been supplied me by N. G. Hutcheson of Boydton, Virginia, Clerk of the Circuit Court of Mecklenburg County, Virginia, and a descendant of Mr. Davis.

The story of this famous racing mare is recounted in a history of Mecklenburg County, Virginia, written by the father of the Mr. Hutcheson who assisted with the gathering of data for this story. *Sportman's Herald and General Stud Book,* by Patrick Nisbett Edgar, lists Polly Williams and her record.

In the Davis barn in Warren County, Polly Williams continued her development and her skill, distinguishing herself particularly at quarter racing. In fact, she became so well known and swept the field so clean that it finally became next to impossible for her owner to obtain a race for her with the other owners of fast horses in that day.

So Mr. Davis kept Polly Williams and enjoyed the personal pleasure that came from seeing her show her heels to the wind—on a track alone. Only a true horse lover can know the thrill that comes with watching such a performance.

And then one day Mr. Davis was faced with the necessity of taking a lengthy business trip that would for many weeks keep him away from Warren County, his plantation there (named "Merry Mount"), and his horse. So he lent his pride and joy, Polly Williams, to a Mr. Johnson, a relative, who lived just across the line from North Carolina in Mecklenburg County, Virginia.

During the protracted absence of Polly Williams' owner, Mr. Johnson did a rather strange thing. He sold the horse to Henry Delony, who also lived in Mecklenburg County. There is no explanation now available for such an unwarranted disposition of a horse that belonged to another. But tradition has it that Mr. Delony did pay a pretty price for the red mare. In fact, the legend is that the price was many times the value of any race horse of that day. Mr. Johnson must have been hard pressed financially to surrender his honor by accepting Delony's fantastic offer.

Mr. Davis's return to Warren County marked the almost simultaneous appearance at the Davis plantation of Delony, who faced Mr. Davis with a challenge for a race. Full of pride for his beloved Polly Williams, Davis promptly accepted the challenge. He told Delony he had a mare that could beat anything on four legs. The race was arranged and a wager made. The bet was five hundred pounds of tobacco —Virginia currency of the day—and the gamble was on a basis of *play-or-pay*. Either party failing to appear with a horse for the contest would thus have to pay as the loser.

This bet was confirmed with a handclasp, and both men mounted saddle horses and rode to the home of one of Mr. Davis's neighbors to draw up the articles of agreement. These preliminaries over, the men parted company. Mr. Davis promptly set out across the Virginia line to the home of his relative to have Polly Williams returned to his barn to begin her training for the race ahead.

Imagine his astonishment and chagrin on arriving at the Johnson home to learn that his beloved Polly Williams had been boldly, illegally, and dishonestly disposed of. The news that his mare was in the hands of Delony must have made Davis's anger complete.

Here was the rightful owner of Polly Williams faced with the fact that he had made a play-or-pay bet against his own horse. He had proposed to race against a mare that he knew in his horse-loving heart could not be beaten by anything running on this continent.

What he said to his relative, Johnson, who had allowed Polly Williams to fall into the hands of the very man, of all others, that he was most unwilling should have her, must have blistered the very earth on the Johnson place. It looked, indeed, as if Davis would lose both his mare and his bet. Time was too short in that day for the slow and lengthy legal technicalities that would be necessary to restore the mare to her rightful owner before the race.

Meantime Delony was paying every attention to Polly and her training. He was seeing that she was well prepared for the race. Whether or not Delony was fully conscious of the dishonesty that was involved in his possession of Polly Williams is a phase of the story not clear after the century and three-quarters that have passed, but it would seem that the very gods themselves conspired to bring about some sort of justice in the case—violent justice though it was.

A period of very bad weather came, and for several days Polly Williams was not taken from her luxurious stall in the Delony barn. She had to forego even so much as the customary walk to the spring where she was normally watered. Instead her food and water were deposited for her in the stall.

And then, on the very eve of the race, the weather broke late one afternoon and the skies cleared. The first thing that Delony ordered after that several days of bad weather was a walk for Polly Williams to the huge crystal spring some distance from the stable for a drink at the horse's favorite watering place. So on that first serene period following several days of stormy weather, Polly Williams, on a halter held by a faithful trainer, stepped high on her way to the spring. It was between dusk and darkness. The clouds had rolled back and the skies cleared just as night began to close in slowly.

Polly Williams lowered her head for the satisfaction of a drink in the spring that she loved.

While the horse was in that position, a rifle, held in some hidden hands, cracked out in the dusk; and a rifle ball plowed through the skull of the illustrious race horse Polly Williams. The wound, caused by an expert shot indeed, was exactly between the horse's eyes. She fell in almost instant death beside the spring.

And thus did Polly Williams end her brilliant career as a race horse. No more would her four white feet fly in the rhythm of the turf. No more would she extend her graceful neck to push a velvet nose across a finish line ahead of her opponents.

In all of her racing career Polly Williams was never defeated. And, even in death, she won for the rightful owner who loved her, for Delony had no horse with which to match Davis; so he had to pay the play-or-pay stakes which Davis claimed.

The fame of Polly Williams was known on many hillsides, and the story of her murder on the eve of a race spread quickly among the colonial lovers of horses. A finger of suspicion pointed to Mr. Davis himself when the full circumstances became known. But it was established to the satisfaction of all that at the moment the rifle shot rang out to kill the horse, Davis was having a dinner party with guests at his own home.

In the years that followed, a story traveled about that Polly Williams was murdered by a Negro slave named Ned, who belonged to Mr. Davis. Ned, a trusted stableman on the Davis plantation, was never questioned or formally charged so far as can be found in any records that have come down from the days of Polly Williams.

Another interesting sidelight on the story of Polly Williams (who, incidentally, bore her breeder's family name— as you see) is that her breeder was a main instigator of the present-day system of horse registration in America. Most of the horses that he owned had long and famous careers and his interest in preserving these records and the records of the lineage of his fine-blooded racers led to today's well-organized system of records in this field.

The Warren County plantation of Mr. Davis later became known as the Pascall Estate. Mr. Davis and Mr. Delony —who laid high stakes on the race that was never run—lived just eight miles apart, one on the North Carolina side of the state line and the other on the Virginia side.

So nearly two centuries after Polly Williams, with her speed and grace, held the limited limelight of her day as a graceful turf performer, we can pay her the tribute that men and women who love horses always like to pay to those superb four-legged animals with almost human intelligence and more than human stamina and performance.

The Strange Killer of Turkey Hollow

WE GO TO Wilkes County for an outdoor mystery, involving hunters, a fine hunting dog, and a "varmint" from the Brushy Mountains that has never been identified further than by that name—"varmint."

The story was first told by a Cabarrus County friend of my newspaper days at Salisbury—W. S. ("Slim") Davis, of Kannapolis, RFD 1.

Our story begins on a certain November day. It was a typically quiet and cold November day in 1944. Frost had painted the leaves of the oak, maple, birch, and hickory of the Brushy Mountains in glowing colors. The creek banks wore frosty beards that sparkled like so many jewels as the red sun came up over Pilot Knob. Its rays touched the Wilkes County hills lightly as Slim Davis and Code Frazier clumped loudly along in their heavy brogans. They were following a narrow wagon road up Turkey Hollow, headed for a day of hunting there near Moravian Falls and Pores Knob.

With the two men was the central character of our story —Jule. She trotted along the frozen ground. Jule belonged to Code Frazier and was a black hound, with white stockings on all four feet, tan dots above her eyes, and a white and tan chest. Her ears would meet under her jaws and she weighed about fifty pounds.

Leaving the narrow road, the little party finally plunged into the woods along the hillside, following Jule as she made her way through the dead brush and leaves. From the very beginning the shooting was good and the hunters had bagged two squirrels before they had been in the woods fifteen minutes. Then Jule suddenly darted forward from a point she was holding, leaped a white pine windfall, and vanished. A squeal, which died instantly, was heard and the hunters knew that Jule had caught one. That made three and the hunt had only begun.

Code and Slim caught up with the hound and took the squirrel that she had for them. As Slim reached down to give the dog an admiring pat, he asked Code—her owner—if she never barked. He realized that they hadn't heard a sound from their long-eared helper since they had started out at sun-up.

Code replied that she never barked except to guide hunters when she became separated from them in her search for game. She had trained herself in that, Code said. And he added the

testimony that she was the smartest dog he had ever known
in his lifetime of owning and following hunting dogs.

Code picked up Jule's foreleg. "See that scar?" he asked
of Slim. "And look at her ears. I don't know *what* done that,
but whatever it was, *it's the only thing that ever whipped
Jule.*"

Slim examined the leg. It had a long ragged scar from
shoulder to knee. It had been a cruel injury but it had healed
nicely. Her ears had been slit in a dozen places, but there was
no way of knowing whether it had been done by a fang or
a claw. Code took a minute of rest to go on with the story,
while they still panted a bit from the climb and the first few
busy moments of hunting. He said Jule never bothered other
dogs and fought only when they jumped on her. A dog hadn't
given Jule those wounds, he said. "Whatever done that
whipped every other dog in the country—and Jule twice."

Code said that he was working in an apple orchard near
that very spot in Turkey Hollow when Jule first jumped *it*.
He said that he lit out for the house to get his gun. There
was some indication to him from the tone of Jule's signaling
bark that it was a fox she had in front of her. She ran whatever it was half a mile beyond the Devil's Smokehouse and
then quit—abruptly. Code said that he followed along with
his gun because he was sure she would pick up the trail again.
But as he drew in near to where he had heard the last sound
from his dog, the silence became more intense and more
prolonged.

And then, just as Code approached Smokehouse rocks, he
met her. Poor old Jule was making her way back, limping
badly, covered with blood, and severely hurt. Code picked
her up and carried her home in his arms. He patched her

wounds and doctored her; after a few weeks of nursing close by the fireside she was well again.

"And," Code said, "whatever that varmint was that she tangled with, she went right back out looking for him again."

It was after several days of running in the fields, regaining her strength and hardening her muscles, that Jule hit the varmint's trail again. She let out a peculiar cry when she did. It was over beyond Snaggy Mountain. Code got his gun and set out in a beeline for the Devil's Smokehouse. He felt sure that the trail would bend in that direction again and that Jule and the varmint might again tangle in the same vicinity where the first fight took place. Code had gotten as far as Shanty Hollow when he heard it.

He had never heard such a fight in all his days, he said. Jule sounded like she was taking something apart and whatever sort of varmint she was fighting, squalled continuously. Code took it at a trot. He wanted to see that thing and he was anxious for a shot at whatever it was that had torn his dog to shreds in a former encounter, and, from the sounds, was repeating the performance.

At this point, the hound interrupted the hunter's story. Jule yawned her boredom at so much talking and so little hunting when the squirrels were so plentiful. Slim suggested that they hunt squirrels again before Jule got disgusted with them and went home.

But Code said with emphasis that Jule not only would never desert a hunting party and return home, but that she would hunt seven days a week. "She is the huntin'est dog that ever hit this country," her owner declared. So the party moved on and brought down several more squirrels before eleven o'clock came and they started to retrace their steps back down Shanty Hollow to Turkey Hollow. After walking in silence for an hour, they came on a comfortable-looking boulder ledge and sat down to smoke as they rested. Jule came in close and dropped at their feet. She knew, of course, that they had stopped hunting. As the men smoked and talked, she suddenly lifted her head, cocked her ears, and edged into the brush. The men, hardly missing her, went on with their stories. After some minutes, Code halted the conversation abruptly to ask where Jule had gone. He looked his worry as he added that Jule always stuck close by him when he started for home.

And then a thin whine sounded down the slope below them, followed by a long-drawn bay. The men looked at each other. Code had troubled eyes. It flashed into his mind that they were near the Devil's Smokehouse again. "That ain't a squirrel she's after," Code said. "But it could be a fox."

Then they heard Jule take off across the side of the hill, yelping in a frenzy of excitement. The echoes caught up her song of the trail—the hunting dog in close pursuit of the quarry. It made music as the Brushy Mountain hills caught up the song of the chase and sent it back and forth from hill to hill. The men stood enthralled, listening. Jule topped the crest of the mountain, swung back to the left of the hunters, and went charging along the ridge above them. She was headed straight for Snaggy Mountain and the Devil's Smokehouse. Code's grim voice snapped them back to reality. "That's no fox either," he said. He pulled his hat down over his right eye. "That's that varmint she's after again."

Whirling about, Code started across the rough terrain at a ponderous gallop. Slim followed, and as they plunged forward in the dry brush they made a great noise. But above it all, they could hear the progress of old Jule's song of the trail as it rang through the hills and the hollows.

The chase circled the rugged slopes and the hunters cut a direct path to the Devil's Smokehouse. Maybe they could get there first this time!

A few minutes later they stood just below the Devil's Smokehouse rocks, a fifty-foot cliff running a quarter of a mile east and west, across the rim of Turkey Hollow. The men held their guns ready for action, watched intently the approaches to that area, and heaved with labored breathing and pounding hearts after the strenuous run.

Jule's song swelled on toward them.

The dog was really taking that varmint to ride, in the hunting vernacular of the hills. Her bell-like voice rang through the ancient hills like a bugle.

Then the hound's song swelled to its highest peak—and abruptly ended.

The men gripped their rifles as they waited for the chase to resume. But only the whisper of the wind in the branches came back to them. "Why don't Jule say something?" Code Frazier, her admiring master, said. "Ole Jule ain't ever acted that way before."

Slim suggested that maybe she had caught the varmint, but Code shook his head. "No. If she had we'd a heard the gol-dangdest fight that ever took place in these hills. Something must'a happened to her. Let's go see."

They followed a faint trail across the hill to where the last sound was heard. At intervals they stopped to listen. Only the wind in the trees, rustling the stubborn dry leaves still hanging on, broke the quiet. Code was frankly worried about his favorite dog. He called and whistled but these noises only bounced back at him.

Then it came to him that Jule might be too badly hurt to answer; so he enlisted Slim's help in searching the entire hillside. Nothing escaped their eyes but they found no trace of the missing dog. Finally it was near dark and they went home, but ignored supper to get Arthur Edsel and his dogs, a blue-ticked foxhound and a redbone, to join the search. They hoped that the dogs would pick up the trail. But these dogs refused to follow a trail, and in the vicinity where the scent was sure to be hot, they only backed into the legs of their masters and refused to leave them. They trembled and whined.

And then suddenly, the blue-ticked hound pointed his slim muzzle at a starlit sky and voiced his protest in a long-drawn, melancholy howl. Instantly the redbone followed suit, and the night was made hideous with the doleful mourning of the animals. The hunters just stared at their dogs, bewildered. They had never known the animals to act like that before.

"That varmint's got 'em buffaloed," Code said grimly.

Finally they all agreed that the dogs were scared and that there was no use to try further to use them on a trail there in the dark Brushy Mountain night. "Let's go home," Code said. He pulled his hat down over his eyes. "We ain't doing no good here a' tall."

So they left Turkey Hollow. The next day Slim Davis had to tell the Fraziers goodbye and return to his Cabarrus County home and to his job at Kannapolis.

In November of the following year, Slim was back again. His first question was about Jule.

Code shook his head slowly and sadly. His dog was never seen again after that November hunt in 1944. Arthur Edsel, Raymond and Willard Lane, Galen Hood, and Reid Anderson had helped in the search for days. They covered the whole region on foot, inch by inch, but never found a thing.

Did they ever find out what the varmint was?

No. But there was a story of how it chased the Lane boys out of Turkey Hollow the next night after Jule disappeared. Then Reid Anderson said that it jumped into the road in front of him as he was coming through the adjoining Shanty Hollow two nights later. Reid said it looked like it was seven feet long. He took a few shots at it with his .38 but seemed to have missed. After that the varmint retired, so far as anyone knows.

That's the story. And it's still an unsolved mystery. Of course, there are theories. One is that several successive forest fires in the Blue Ridge in 1942 and 1943 drove a lot of the wildlife, including bear and deer, over into the Brushies and along the Yadkin River valley. In that migratory flight from the fire a panther may have left his usual habitat and come to the Brushies to make his home. That is perhaps the best guess as to what it was that tangled with brave and persistent old Jule—a true hunting dog to the end.

The Baffling Mountain Balds

THE Bald Mountain mystery is the second botanical curiosity in this group of North Carolina stories. It is as old as the memory of man in Western North Carolina, and as old as descriptive records. The mystery of the bald mountains continues to be just as much of a mystery as ever in spite of some neat and rather convincing solutions that have been advanced in recent years.

The Bald Mountain mystery is this: Certain Appalachian mountain tops in Western North Carolina, from 2,000 to 6,000 feet high, will not support the growth of trees and have come to attract special attention as a group of bald mountain tops, devoid of timber or even small trees.

Altitude—or the timber line—is not the answer. Both Mount Mitchell and Clingman's Dome, each of them nearly 7,000 feet high, are timbered right up to the very top. But the bald mountains refuse to support the growth of trees, in the same mountainous section, although some of them are as much as 5,000 feet lower and nearer to sea level.

There they stand: Craggy Bald, Big Bald (sometimes called Grier's Bald), Hoopers Bald, Andrew's Bald, Wayah Bald, Mount Sterling, Rumbling Bald, Roan Mountain, Standing Indian, Gregory Bald, Parsons Bald, Cheoah Bald, Heintooga Bald, and so on. Between Mount Guyot and Clingman's Dome is a whole region of so-called heath balds.

These treeless mountain tops scattered throughout Western North Carolina stand there in the midst of heavy spruce and hardwood growths. Locally the bald-topped mountains are called "hells," "woolly-heads," and "slicks"—the latter because from a distance the dense growth of grass or shrubs that covers the treeless mountain tops appears to be a smooth covering, made to look even more so because the short growth has a uniform height. In these areas, where apparently the trees have been eliminated, grasses and small shrub growth have obtained such a fast hold that they have been able to choke out tree seedlings in all the years since.

Big Bald is sometimes called Grier's Bald in honor of David Grier who lived as a hermit there from 1802 to 1834 after having been rejected by the daughter of Colonel David Vance. He became involved in disputes when settlers began moving into the area and killed a man. Although Grier was acquitted on the grounds of insanity, he was later slain by one of his victim's friends, but not, however, until after he had published a pamphlet explaining why he had taken the law into his own hands.

Craggy Bald, famous for the shallow floral covering of its dome, which is devoid of trees of any kind, has the largest known stand of purple rhododendron. The shrub is so dense over miles of this area that in the flowering season the blooms form a solid blanket of rich rose and purple.

Near Deals Gap on the North Carolina–Tennessee boundary and at the western extremity of the Great Smoky Mountains National Park is Gregory Bald, and from the top of its dome, standing nearly 5,000 feet above sea level, a good view can be had of Parsons Bald to the west and Cheoah Bald to the south. The Cherokees called Gregory Bald Tsistuyi (meaning the rabbit place). Here, according to the Indians, the rabbits had their "town houses," and here lived their chief, the Great Rabbit, who was as large as a deer.

Heintooga Bald, also known as Flat Creek Bald, in the Waynesville–Soco Gap region, offers a view to the south of the main divide of the Smokies from Clingman's Dome to Mount Guyot.

In the Highlands and Deep Gap area is Wayah Bald, a little more than 5,000 feet in elevation, and one of the highest mountains in Eastern America, whose summit is reached by a motor road. The John B. Byrne tower was erected on Wayah Bald in 1937, as a memorial to a former supervisor of Nantahala National Forest, and from this tower views are available in all directions. The valley far below is marked with the sharp curves of the Little Tennessee River.

Rumbling Bald is in the Lake Lure area. It is the long mountain range that towers above the lake, and it received its name from the fact that thunderous rumbling sometimes emanates from it. Faults exist among the rocks, and landslips have exposed caves high up on the slopes.

And so we have this scattered group of bald mountains in Western North Carolina. They are similar in appearance and apparently in the source of their mysterious bareness. All are a part of the general unsolved mystery of how and why they became and remain bald when trees grow in dense and primeval forests all about them.

In 1938 W. A. Gates of Louisiana State University discovered twig gall wasps laying their eggs in oak trees on mountain tops, which eventually killed the timber. He concluded that the wasps were the real barbers of the bald mountains, keeping the growth on their topknots cut back with the perfection of some giant barber with monster clippers.

But Dr. B. W. Wells, botanist at N. C. State College, stuck to his theory that certain mountain tops were favored camping spots for the Indians, who continually burned off the tops to furnish space for their villages and to provide themselves with unobstructed lookout points.

Dr. Wells has pointed out that the balds are without exception gently sloping tops—not steep or rugged or precipitous—and that they are also usually on the southern, or protected, side of a slope, and that often strong flowing springs are conveniently near. In other words, these bald mountain tops were all ideal tenting grounds for the aborigines.

Dr. Wells has said that after a fire in the mountains, the

arboreal succession is of "fire cherry," which under repeated fire succeeds itself in basal shoot regeneration. Thus, he concludes, natural fire itself cannot explain the balds, and hence the grass sub-climax must result from human—and that is to say Indian—interference.

Recently it was discovered that a great belt of olivine underlies the bald mountain section, and some geologists have pointed out that the ore had a very shallow overburden. They then advanced a theory that the soil was too thin and poor to support trees.

Whatever the cause, the balds have existed since earliest explorations and seem exempt from the usual forest succession, which normally would cover them with pines in from five to twenty years, to be succeeded by the inevitable oak and hickory or oak and chestnut forests.

These barren-top mountains vary widely in composition. Grassy balds are fairly common, and often quite large, and sometimes are used as summer pastures by cattlemen. On some balds such as Mount Sterling, the sedges predominate. Still others are favored by wild flowers, such as the exquisite little bluet. The shrub balds are usually covered with rhododendron, and, on the lower levels, laurel, and this usually forms a dense covering so thick as to be almost impenetrable.

Craggy Gardens near Asheville is the most famous of the shrub-covered balds. Thousands of visitors flock there to see the display that this roundtop puts on each June.

The Roan Mountain bald, one of the more beautiful of the treeless mountain tops, is covered with green alder. Other balds are dominated by such shrubs as beaked hazelnut, azalea, shrub honeysuckle, and laurel in predominance in the lower altitudes. The hypothesis is that, once the grasses and shrubs come firmly in, the trees are unable to force their way back up the slopes.

In addition to their park-like appearance and colorful blossoms, the balds offer another advantage to sightseers. They provide points from which the most spectacular views of mountain scenery can be had because they contain no obstructing timber.

There is a romantic substantiation for the Wells theory that these mountain tops are bald today because of repeated clearances by the Indians, using fire. This is borne out in Cherokee mythology. The story is told about the Standing Indian bald but can of course be applied to them all.

Years ago, according to the Cherokee legend, on the banks of the Little Tennessee River, near Nikwasi, an awful beast with widespread wings and beady eyes plunged suddenly from the sky, and seized and carried away an Indian child. And such raids were repeated, there and elsewhere, until the people were completely terrorized. So the Indians cleared the mountain tops, undoubtedly by burning them off, to make lookouts there. The den of the marauder was finally discovered on the south slope of a certain peak, inaccessible even to the most dauntless hunter. So the Indians appealed to their Great Spirit, and he heard their pleas and sent thunder and lightning against the monster and destroyed it. But ever after that, even until this day, the mountain top has remained a treeless bald.

Standing Indian received its name because a warrior stationed as a sentinel against the depredating monster deserted his post when the destroying bolt of lightning flashed through the sky. For this defection he was turned to stone and still appears there, standing, a dismal figure, in eternal vigil.

Dr. Wells's theory perhaps comes nearer to offering a solution for the long-existing "riddle of the balds." But the riddle is still considered unsolved.

The Missing Major

NORTH CAROLINA also has its present-day unsolved mysteries. Typical of these, and one of the most baffling, is the story of Major Robert R. Clark.

The Major Clark case is of World War II vintage and has to do with a soldier who left Raleigh in his car for Fayetteville and—for all anyone has ever been able to learn—melted into thin air.

Bespectacled Major Clark, a former newspaper man, was attached to headquarters of the Southeastern Defense Command at Raleigh in 1944. He was thirty-three years old at the time and lived in the home of John A. Park, publisher of the *Raleigh Times,* and Mrs. Park, and he was on a mission to Fort Bragg when the disappearance—since veiled in complete mystery—took place. Few of the riddles the youthful Major left behind him have been solved. Many deepen with the passage of time.

Major Clark was a military-minded man, his landlord, Publisher Park, has said. Military associates said he was efficient.

The many odd features of the case have compelled the interest of amateur and professional sleuths alike. Obviously, the solution does not lie along ordinary lines of investigation. Routine methods, diligently applied, have produced nothing to indicate whether the Major was murdered, committed suicide after hiding his car, or deliberately chose a dramatic way of stepping completely out of his identity to begin life anew.

It was not the type of disappearance that might be explained by amnesia. Either Clark disappeared by design, was murdered, or was possibly kidnapped. Investigators agree on these points.

So far as known, Major Clark was last seen in Raleigh at a Fayetteville Street luncheonette, near the Capitol, at midday of March 17, 1944. He told a fellow-officer that he intended to leave at once for Fort Bragg in his own Dodge coupe, and then return to Raleigh to prepare for a sixteen-day tour of duty to army camps in the Southeastern area. His manner was entirely normal. There was no hint of anything weighing on his mind. He got up, paid the cashier, opened the door, and stepped into what has become one of the state's deepest mysteries.

Seventy-two hours later, when the Major failed to keep an appointment with a lieutenant and a private who had been assigned to accompany him on his official trip, Army authorities listed him as AWOL and ordered a search for him. Police were notified, and a description of the missing man, along with the license number of his 1941 Dodge coupe, was broadcast over the North Carolina highway patrol's radio system.

The major was described as five feet, nine inches tall, having dark brown hair (closely cropped), dark brown eyes, sharp features, and wearing metal-rimmed eyeglasses. The insignia of the New York–Philadelphia sector, Eastern Defense Command, appeared on a shoulder patch of his uniform.

Two days after the search began a letter addressed to Clark was received in Raleigh. It was a letter from a Kansas City girl whom Clark had been courting for more than a year—the kind of letter any soldier might be glad to receive from his best girl. The writer expressed her joy at Clark's having found himself so happily situated in Raleigh, and banteringly broached the subject of their getting married.

New Jersey detectives interviewed the writer of the letter, Miss Catherine Swanson, in the hope of finding a clue in the private life of Major Clark, but Miss Swanson could shed no light on the mystery. She had met Clark in New York and they had seen a great deal of each other. They had spoken of marriage, but no definite plans had been made. Clark, she said, had been in the habit of writing to her at least once a week.

Miss Swanson recalled that frequently she talked with Clark by long distance telephone and had tried to reach him a few hours after he had presumably left for Fort Bragg.

Probing further into the Major's background, investigators

learned that he had worked for ten years as a reporter on the Bergen (N. J.) *Evening Record* before joining the Army in 1940. Employees of the paper remembered him as a competent, highly intelligent newsman, quiet-mannered, agreeable, well-liked but reserved and uncommunicative about his private affairs. He had never been in serious trouble nor was he known to have formed any romantic attachment.

In Raleigh and Fort Bragg, army officers who had been acquainted with Major Clark could give no information that might clear up the case. They were unanimous in pooh-poohing the suggestion that the Major might have arranged his disappearance to escape his duties as an officer. There was nothing in his record to indicate he had ever felt dissatisfied with Army life.

Questioned regarding the Major's attitude toward the Army as revealed in his letters to her, Miss Swanson said "the Army meant everything" to him. He was eager to do whatever job lay before him, but might have preferred active duty in Europe.

Clark, who in 1935 became a lieutenant in the New Jersey National Guard, was skilled in marksmanship and an expert on firearms. He had won three medals for sharpshooting.

In the early stages of the investigation, the possibility of Clark's having suffered from amnesia or some other mental illness appeared frequently in police theories. Relatives recalled that he had twice been hard hit by tragedy. As a youth he had discovered the body of his father, a suicide, hanging from a wall-fixture, and the shock plunged him into a long period of depression. Again, on the death of his mother a few years later he had been inconsolable.

Other facts gleaned in initial inquiries tended to set at rest the suspicion that Clark might have contrived his own disappearance. It was learned he had maintained checking accounts in Raleigh and New York, but had withdrawn no large sum from either. The Dodge coupe was his own property and unencumbered. He was on the best of terms with the girl he evidently intended to marry. He was financially well off, and apparently eager to help win the war. There seemed no reason for his wanting to disappear.

The search for Clark continued without let-up. The highway patrol radioed his description three times a day for two weeks. The Federal Bureau of Investigation, State Bureau of Investigation, county and city police joined forces in trying to solve his puzzling disappearance. Military police all over the country were on the lookout for him, and Army pilots at Pope Field and Camp Butner were ordered to make aerial checks of rural sections between Raleigh and Fayetteville.

With seemingly every theory exhausted, the investigation bogged down and the case came to be spoken of as the "perfect" disappearance.

Then, exactly seven months after the Major had vanished, a break occurred which galvanized law officers into renewed activity.

While game-hunting with his dogs in a densely wooded section of Hoke County, about two miles from Montrose, Robert Parks discovered a Dodge coupe almost completely covered over with leaves, pine-brush, vines, and army blankets. Sheriff Dave Hudgin was notified and sped to the scene. The New Jersey license plate on the weather-beaten car indicated that it was the long-sought Dodge belonging to Major Clark.

Civilian and military authorities made a thorough examination of the coupe and the personal effects it contained. Several articles of clothing were strewn on the ground near the machine, which in the obscure setting, could not be distinctly seen at a distance of more than fifteen feet. Somebody— possibly Clark himself—had done a highly ingenious and most effective job of camouflaging the coupe. Military authorities who saw the concealed car said it was the work of an expert, well trained in camouflage. Great pains had been taken with the job.

Wrapped in underwear in the smallest of three handbags was a .22 calibre automatic pistol identified as the property of the missing Major and in the car lay a .30 calibre Springfield rifle. Most of the other articles were thought to have belonged to Clark. There was no accounting for a woman's small valise which was found near the car cache.

Seven months of neglect in the changing weather had reduced the cream-colored coupe to a dilapidated condition. The tires were still partly inflated but insects and vermin had left their mark on mildewed clothing, luggage, and other articles, all of which had greatly deteriorated during the months the car had been hidden. Sheriff Hudgin was of the opinion that the coupe had been concealed in the thicket since the day Clark disappeared.

The surrounding countryside was searched by soldiers from near-by Camp MacKall, Boy Scouts, and civilian volunteers, but no clue was unearthed to indicate what had befallen the Major. The finding of the automobile aided detectives only in a negative way. It seemed to dispose of the amnesia theory, but contributed nothing toward ultimate solution of the mystery. In fact, the woman's handbag found near the auto had the effect of further confusing the already muddled case.

Friends of Major Clark recalled that he had often picked up hitchhikers, both civilians and men in uniform, and it could reasonably be supposed that he had been the victim of some stranger thus befriended. However, the cunning with which the coupe had been camouflaged was suggestive of Army methods. Such a ruse might have occurred to the Major himself, versed as he was in Army subtleties. Also, remembering that Clark had twice suffered acute melancholy, some investigators suggested that Clark had hidden the car and then committed suicide elsewhere in an equally fantastic way.

The search for Major Clark became nation-wide, with newspapers and wire-services carrying accounts of the case. An insurance company with which Clark held a policy ordered its ace investigator to devote his full time to tracking down rumors. At Salisbury he tried without success to get a line on an unofficial report that an Army Major answering Clark's description had been seen in the company of a young woman waiting for a north-bound train. None of the tips bore fruit.

One novel theory, however far-fetched, received attention. The favorite dodge of fiction writers to hide their "wanted" criminals under phony identities in the one place they are sure to be free of police pursuit—in jail—was considered. Could an Army man hide himself in the Army? Could Major Clark have hoaxed authorities into believing that he was dead and then used his knowledge of Army procedure to forge enlistment papers and get the overseas service he desired? The war is over. Military wheels, like those of the gods, grind slow, but grind exceedingly fine. Sooner or later fingerprints, physical examinations, discharge—something would have given him away.

So the "case of the missing Major" remains shrouded in mystery, with police and private investigators apparently no nearer a solution than they were in 1944 when the Major disappeared.

In November, 1945, an offer that $2,000 would be paid for information as to the whereabouts of the Major, dead or alive, was made by Guy H. Castle of Chicago, Clark's uncle by marriage. Mr. Castle said: "Both Mrs. Castle and I feel that if there is any possibility of solving this mystery through personal efforts, we should not overlook any detail that might lead to a clue."

A committee of three Raleigh citizens was named to rule upon claims for the reward if the case was solved. Composing the committee were Graham Andrews, then mayor of Raleigh; John A. Park, Sr., editor of the *Raleigh Times;* and LeRoy Martin, vice-president of the Wachovia Bank and Trust Company, the firm which was to handle payment of the reward.

Months passed and the $2,000 "bait" attracted nothing. It proved to be no lure whatever to any person who might have come forward with a clue. Finally the Castles gave up and reclaimed the cash that had been placed on deposit in the Wachovia Bank in Raleigh for payment of the reward.

The mystery has only increased as time passes.

Is Major Robert R. Clark, thirty-three years old when he dropped out of sight, dead or alive today? Army Intelligence, State Highway Patrol, Federal Bureau of Investigation, State Bureau of Investigation, insurance investigators, and others have been, and still are, asking that question.

Among them all, and with their combined talents, they have been able to shed no light whatever on the strange disappearance. If he was murdered or was a suicide, where is the body? If he sought to disappear, why did he take no money from his bank accounts and leave all personal effects behind? Why was the car so painstakingly concealed with the most expert army camouflage methods—hidden alike from the ground and from the air?

These are the still unanswered questions in the case of the missing major.

The Unknown Rhymster

SOME mysteries get their solution—finally. While most of those presented in this Tar Heel collection are still enigmas, there have been some solutions and explanations.

Our North Carolina mysteries include at least one in the realm of literature—and it was solved after a century of searching for the answer.

During that period of more than a hundred years the puzzle that persisted in our North Carolina literature was this: Who wrote *Attempts at Rhyming*, "by an Old Field Teacher"?

Published late in 1839, *Attempts at Rhyming* carefully cloaked its author in anonymity. The little volume came from the press of the Raleigh *Star*, owned by Thomas J. Lemay in the early 1800's. In announcing publication of the book the *Star* said (in its issue for December 4, 1839) that the author was a "gentleman of high literary and classical attainments, of great moral worth; and as a flattering evidence of public regard, we observe on the list of subscribers of his work, the names of the most distinguished literary characters of the state."

Obviously, the pioneer days and times of the early 1830's did not provide too many gentlemen "of high literary and classical attainments." Such a gentleman might have been easily identified. But this was not the case. The mystery was complete.

When the book appeared, its literary value was immediately recognized. The Raleigh *Standard,* another state capital newspaper of that day, said of the volume of verse and its mysterious author that "it certainly exhibits no inconsiderable degree of poetical talent. He has, we think been very successful."

For its day the little volume apparently received a nice promotion and was helped with considerable advertising. The Raleigh *Microcosm* proclaimed in May of 1840 the volume of poetry "for sale at Mr. Tucker's store, the *Star* office, and at Mr. De Carteret's."

Down over the years that have followed, judgment was repeatedly passed on the collection of poems, and it was always favorable. But still the identity of the poet himself or herself was not revealed. No one came forward to receive in person the plaudits that the rhyming brought. The writing was good; the poetry had its popularity; the effort was favorably received. Even in later years the volume has had its readers.

Those who have read the little book have with one accord agreed that the unidentified poet was a genuine scholar. Reference to scholarly things, quotations from Latin, French, and Italian, insight into the problems of the day all indicate the scholarly mind of the poet.

His lines reveal many things—if not the name or the identity of the rhymster. From the pages of *Attempts at Rhyming* we see that the writer was either a Catholic or had a preference for the Catholic church. The lines reflect extensive travel through the wide geographical range that is covered in the poems themselves. Some of them carry dates and places of their composition—such as "London, 1820," "Rome, 1822," "New York, 1822," and again "London, 1830."

He knew and loved home, too. He wrote of North Carolina as well as of foreign parts. One poem, called "On Chapel Hill," reveals his love and his knowledge of the place:

> Wood-creasted hills and verdant vales among,
>   See Northern-Carolina's learn'd retreat!
> Where arts and letters and the poet's song
>   Adorn with majesty the Muses' seat.

The elusive rhymster has one complete romantic narrative of 58 pages in the volume. The setting is the Alps and the lovers who are central characters make their way through robber bands, duels, and the complications of mistaken identity, finally to arrive at a satisfactory union of sweethearts.

Copies of *Attempts at Rhyming* are rare things today. The University of North Carolina Library had one that was lost many years ago and was not replaced until 1939, when another copy was obtained. The present copy in the University Library was purchased from the books of the late Professor W. K. Boyd of Duke University.

With the arrival of the Professor Boyd copy of *Attempts at Rhyming* at the University Library, the first clue leading to the discovery of the identity of the "Old Field Teacher" developed.

Until then the literary mystery had persisted. At about that time Bruce Cotten, the well-known Baltimore collector of North Caroliniana, was writing that the "Old Field Teacher's" identity remained "concealed in spite of painstaking research." Hight C. Moore, a careful student of North Carolina poetry, wrote that the unidentified poet was one "whose identity the most persistent efforts have failed to disclose."

And then someone noticed an inscription on the fly leaf of the copy of *Attempts at Rhyming* that the University of North Carolina Library had obtained from among the books of Professor Boyd. Written there was:

"John C. Haskell from his teacher, A. Hart."

Could "A. Hart" be the "Old Field Teacher?" There was a teacher by that name who gave instruction in North Carolina in the early 1800's. His full name was Alban J. X. Hart. He operated the Shocco Classical Seminary at Shocco Springs, in Warren County, in 1839. In that decade Shocco Springs was the most fashionable resort and watering place in North

Carolina. It was ten miles from Warrenton and was considered more or less reserved for the aristocracy.

And so the hitherto-little-noticed autograph in the Boyd copy of *Attempts* set off a chain of literary investigations and deductions. Interested students of North Carolina poetry started tracking down all available information about Hart.

The hunt led to the William Gaston Papers deposited in the Southern Historical Collection in the University of North Carolina Library. In that collection are two unpublished letters that led to the final discovery of the Old Rhymster's identity. The letters represent an exchange of correspondence between Alban J. X. Hart and Judge William Gaston of New Bern, and they establish without doubt the fact that Hart and the Rhymster were one and the same person.

One of the young North Carolina writers and critics who gave some close study to a solution of the literary mystery was Richard Walser, author of *North Carolina in the Short Story,* and a professor of English at N. C. State College. After the identity was established, Professor Walser also dug into the available materials and came up with a brief story of the life of the poet. He found that Alban J. X. Hart was born in England about 1798. He was educated at Stonyhurst College, the oldest Catholic public school in England. Entering the novitiate, he studied for a while in Rome, but ill health forced him to abandon his intention of becoming a priest. On his return to England he became a master at Sedgley Park School.

After some difficulties with church authorities, Hart left England and came to the United States.

In January, 1838, he was principal of the Oxford Male Academy, one of the most prominent schools of the day. He was described as a "gentleman of considerable attainments in classical and scientific knowledge, acquired in England, Italy, and France."

Hart left Oxford and in the following summer he corresponded with Judge William Gaston of New Bern.

After the publication of *Attempts at Rhyming*, there is nothing known of the poet's activities in North Carolina. In 1853 a New York firm published a book of his, *The Mind and Its Creations: An Essay on Mental Philosophy*. And in 1860 in Baltimore, A. Hart brought out the second edition of an *English Grammar for Beginners*.

Eventually he returned to England and resided at St. Mary's College, Oscott, to which was presented his library of scientific and classical books. In London, he reissued his verses under the title which in the North Carolina volume had been his most noteworthy effort, *The Hermit of the Alps, and Other Poems*. On April 13, 1879, he died at Worcester, aged eighty-one.

At last, after more than a century, the mask is down. We know the name of "Old Field Teacher," and a North Carolina literary mystery is solved.